Zombie Girl
3
Retribution

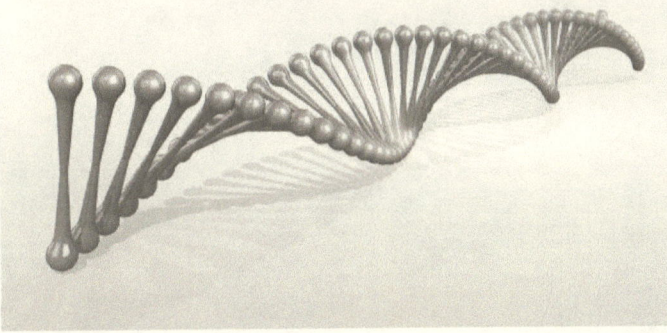

Zombie Girl 3 Retribution

Copyright © 2018 by Elle Klass
ISBN - 978-0-9992504-7-1
Published by Books by Elle, Inc.
Cover art created by TL Katt
Editor Dawn Lewis Bookmarks Editing
For more information go to
http://elleklass.weebly.com/
Blog: http://thetroubledoyster.blogspot.com
Facebook:
https://www.facebook.com/ElleKlass
Twitter- @elleklass

Author's Disclaimer

Books in the Zombie Girl Series

Premonition
Infection
Retribution

Other Books by Elle

As Snow Falls

Bloodseeker Series
The Vampires next Door
The Monster Upstairs
The Ghost Within

Baby Girl Series
In the Beginning Book I
Moonlighting in Paris Book II
City by the Bay Book III
Bite the Big Apple Book IV
Caribbean Heat Book V
Return to the Bay Book VI
Prison of the Past Book VII
Baby Girl Box Set -Books I - IV

Zombie Girl 3 Retribution

Chapter One

Somewhere in the Atlantic Ocean Jack and Bryce

J ack sat with his feet propped on the dash of
the navigation board in the cockpit of his
recently acquired, built for speed, sleek yacht.
It didn't matter that, technically, he stole it since
whoever owned it had most likely turned zombie
and was now stacked in one of the piles in
Casablanca.

His mind tingled and itched with curiosity as he
considered everything that had transpired over the
past few weeks. It was difficult for him to grasp first
of all that people were turning into flesh-eating
monsters. Next was all the commotion with the huge
storm in the Atlantic, which surprised him they'd
survived, then Mt. Vesuvius blowing its lid when
they were trapped in the sea below. The tsunami it
caused grounded their small boat. How they
survived all that blew his mind and he was
convinced it was divine intervention. Nevertheless,
they were running out of lives and sooner or later
zombies, a natural disaster, or something else just as
devastating would kill them.

What bothered him the most didn't have
anything to do with death or the many times he'd
risked his life over such a short period of time. It
was the loss of modern conveniences. While in the
Atlantic the cell phone service went out and so did

radio and communication. Maybe it could be explained reasonably since they were miles away from towers but orbiting the Earth were more satellites than he had hairs on his arms and, in today's world -- or maybe yesterday's pre-zombie world -- those suckers controlled everything.

What couldn't be reasonably explained was the lack of electricity in Italy and Morocco. Maybe one city or even small country, but both? Neither country had power. To him that was more than coincidence. It was an impossibility. These weren't third world countries and he didn't doubt their residents enjoyed the conveniences provided by electricity, so why did it suddenly stop?

He scratched his bald head in contemplation. Surrounding them was nothing but the wide open Atlantic. He couldn't even see the U.S. military carrier they were following. He stayed just behind the huge wake caused by the propulsion of the large ship, breaking a serious boating rule, but he didn't figure rules and laws applied anymore. He hoped to catch a little speed, save a bit of gas and, most importantly, didn't want to lose the ship until he was positive it was headed to Norfolk, VA.

The world was round and, since they were on the ocean, one couldn't see more than a few miles in any one direction unless, of course, standing at some height above the water. The carrier had heights that made it possible for them to see further than a few miles over the surface and equipment that furthered that reach.

He wasn't using any fancy gadgets and the wake of the large ship, he hoped, would camouflage them enough the military wouldn't know they were following. Of course there was always radar and he was sure they had theirs on. It was a risk he was willing to take for now. The military's involvement in this scenario was both encouraging and discouraging. They were, without a doubt, responsible for halting cell phone service and it wasn't a reach to say they had a hand in stopping electricity. *But why? What was their motivation?*

Feeling relatively safe, his mind was in a far-off spot and he didn't hear Bryce walk into the cockpit. He didn't notice him until he shoved his legs and said, "I don't need your feet in my face."

"Huh?" Jack queried as he turned his head to face Bryce, his long chestnut hair pulled back in the usual ponytail. "Uh, yeah." Jack collapsed his feet from the dash.

"How long you think it will take to cross the ocean?"

"Not as long as it would if we weren't in the wake of the ship," Jack answered, knowing the stream gave the yacht a little extra oomph. "Like dolphins, it conserves energy and gets us where we want faster."

Bryce nodded. He'd never thought of that, but hadn't spent enough time in the ocean until the last few weeks to even think about it. The intercoastal waterways is where he'd spent most his time boating and on occasion in the Atlantic, off the coast of Florida, deep sea fishing with his father. When he saw a dolphin he marveled at it but didn't consider much else.

"What's got your mind?" Jack's silence since boarding the boat had Bryce curious.

Grabbing a toothpick from the pack he'd found in the galley, Jack stuffed it in his mouth and chewed. In nervous times it helped him concentrate. "Lots of things that don't make sense."

Bryce grinned and chuckled, nothing in the past few weeks made any sense, not to a rational person. "Like?"

"Losing cell service and Mr. Smyth's explanation of GPS makes sense. Right, it's an easy way to target those living, but why lose service? And why no electricity?" Jack swished the toothpick to the other side of his mouth.

Bryce smoothed a few loose strands of hair back. "Guess there's no one to run it?" He was a smart kid but at a loss for why nothing worked. He could only assume.

Jack shook his head. "Isn't much in our pre-zombie world that needed human hands to make it go, everything is automated. Humans simply keep it working when something goes wrong."

Both men stared ahead at the vast ocean, perplexed, for several minutes before Bryce broke the silence. "We live on our phones and without them we're trapped in an outdated world without common conveniences or any way to communicate. It's like living in a bubble."

Jack considered his words and they made a heck of a lot of sense. "That's it! I think you're on to something. We need our conveniences and lived in a world spoiled with them. Take them away and we don't know how to survive, at least not for long. Some will adapt, but most will give in at a promise of their old life, or something resembling it."

It all became clear to Bryce at that second. "The military. They did it. Cut off access to the world, communication and conveniences we use daily, and people will go willingly. With the promise of food and as you said 'something resembling their old life' they won't fight. That carrier is loaded with survivors like us. Some fought it but most boarded without a complaint."

Jack gave him a half-cocked smile. "I think you nailed it. The military, or whatever semblance of government the U.S. has. Or possibly its bigger. Maybe world leaders have joined forces and are collecting all the survivors."

"But why? Isn't life about free will?"

Jack sniggered. "Those people turned zombie lost their free will the minute they took sick. Now they're mindless deaders. Not every country has the freedoms we spoiled Americans have and in rough times we lose some of those freedoms. It's called Martial Law."

Their conversation paused for a second, giving way to silence as the yacht purred quiet as a kitten. A large bird flew over them, flapping sideways, then dipped into the water beside the boat and came back up with a fish in its mouth. Its wings fluttered haphazardly as it coasted away from them. They watched in curiosity and jumped when a scratching sound grabbed their attention.

They'd gotten too cozy. Bryce jumped into zombie slashing mode, bounced out of his seat and lunged for the shovel he'd propped against the wall earlier. "You heard that?"

Jack nodded and grabbed his handy rifle that proved solid in killing zombies. Padding slowly out of the cockpit and onto the deck, they followed the noise, locating where it was coming from.

"I think it's coming from downstairs," offered Bryce. Quite a few years younger, his senses and reaction times were quicker than Jack's.

Jack swallowed. He hadn't checked the engine room. It wasn't a large area and he didn't think a mindless zombie would go down there. They were drawn to noise and living humans as a food source. The boat, sitting quiet in the dock, had neither. Yet the sound was quiet, barely audible over the engine. Not something caused by a full-grown human. Then a terrifying thought struck him, maybe it was a child whose parents put it there for safety.

Chapter Two

Maddie

I swung around after searching the shocked and frightened faces of my mother and extended family including Katrina, Bryce's mother, and his sister Melissa. My father was the only one not in the room and two sets of footsteps meant someone else was with him.

Standing in the doorway with my father was a tall man. Dark-framed glasses with extra thick lenses magnified his eyes so they looked as if they were bulging from the sockets, the left lens cracked like a spider web. A navy blue shirt wrapped his chest snuggly and rose over his pants displaying the donut roll of fat around his belly. His pants fit him the opposite; instead of tight, they hung loose around his waist, threatening at any minute to drop to his ankles.

In his hand he held a gun pointed towards my father's head. My eyes widened, but not in fear. That had left me sometime in Italy. Anger roused me now. After everything we went through, especially my dad fighting off the zombie virus or whatever it was, I couldn't let him die now. I had to think quick.

His shaky hand was close to the trigger. I took a breath and slid my eyes across the gun. A metal piece in the back was up. My limited experience with guns -- I shuddered remembering the first time I shot one. A phantom ache in my thigh reminded me of the experience. My mind raced through him pushing the trigger and stopped when it didn't budge because of the metal piece. It wouldn't fire. At least I thought so. I was confident enough that my head switched gears and scanned the room searching for a way to stop him.

"I won't hurt him, but I need everyone to take a seat, hands under your butts." His dark skin and hair gave away he was of African descent but his voice had a British ring to it like Heather's and was higher pitched. He sounded like a frightened girl.

My mom, who was in a conversation with Katrina, sat across from her on the plush bench. Little Melissa cuddled around her mother. Sarah gawked at me wide-eyed. Her eyes shifting from him to me. She knew me well. This wasn't OK and I had to do something to stop it. Bennet swallowed hard, his eyes fixed on the man as he slowly sat down on a stool. I felt Heather's eyes on my back.

"You too." He waved the gun at me with his shaky hand.

I sped my steps and scooted backwards until I reached the bench Heather sat on and lowered myself.

"This vessel is now enroute for Cape Town. That is my home and my family is still there. You are going to help me get them out of there and bring them to safety." There was no fluctuation in his words unlike his eyes and the shakiness in his hand. He meant business.

I cringed. Cape Town would add days to our journey. Days we couldn't afford. It was important we got back to Jacksonville and found the WEAC facility.

My mother spoke up and was a bit snarky with her words, making me proud, "There's no need for guns. We're all healthy and living," she stressed the last word, "humans and still have passion and will in our hearts. We would gladly help you."

The man's eyes shifted towards her. Without lowering the gun he said, "I trust no one." Beads of sweat formed below his hairline and that's when I noted how pallid his skin was.

My butt hit the cushion and something hard pushed against my left butt cheek. The man's eyes on my mother across the small room, I strolled my hand over the cushion and lowered my fingers to the back and beneath, curling them around the object. It was round and firm -- a ball. Slowly I slid it out, keeping it between my curled fingers.

Sarah shifted her glance to me then cleared her throat a couple times like something was stuck in it. Suddenly she started a coughing fit, rolling her torso over her lap. He waved the gun towards my mom. "Make her stop!" He was seriously getting on my nerves. Weapons were meant for deaders, not healthy living people. If we killed each other, then who'd rebuild the world? Certainly not the deaders.

My mom stood and rushed to Sarah's aid while I rolled the ball in my hand and raised it. The man still focused on Sarah who was fully bent over, coughing as if she was dying. My mother smoothing her hair.

"She needs water," my mom stated.

"Do it!" he ordered, his nose wrinkling as if in disgust.

My mom scurried towards the doorway that led to the galley.

Throwing had never been a strength of mine. The only athletic bones in my body started and ended with slashing zombies. Regardless, I let go of the ball with force, aiming for his head. My stomach clutched and my breath caught as the ball released and sailed through the air.

"Where are you--" the man's words cut off abruptly, followed with a yelp that erupted from his chest when the ball didn't hit the man's head but sailed into the wall. My heart sank, then out of nowhere as if he apported, an orange streak of fluff soared through the air and clung to the man's arm. He dropped the weapon and spun to get Cat off his arm, but his claws were dug into his flesh so deep that Cat spun with him. His back legs flailed in the air then clamped onto the man's chest. A deep growl rose in the animal's throat as the man fought.

In the commotion the gun clattered as it fell and my father kicked it with his foot as he stepped to the side. It rolled to a stop against Sarah's foot. She grabbed it and immediately stopped coughing, threw her torso upward then stood, pointing the gun at the man. For someone who'd never shot a gun, she held it like a pro.

Cat climbed from his arm and jumped over the man's shoulder. Blood drizzled over the man's arm, dropping to the floor, and his shirt was ripped bare in the front. I never figured Cat for an attack cat but

11

was never more happy I brought him along than at that moment.

Cat scrambled to Sarah and rubbed against her leg as if she summoned him and it was team work. She sauntered toward the man who backed up until he hit the wall. The gun, aimed at his head, in Sarah's steady hand.

"We didn't survive a tsunami and deaders to die at your hand. Who do you think you are sneaking onto our boat?" Sarah steadily walked towards him until the gun was against the flesh of his sweaty and bloody chest. The room was silent except for Sarah's voice and the steady rhythm of our heartbeats as we watched in angst and surprise.

Sarah wasn't a violent person. She wanted to be a vet, but maybe a cat whisperer was a better occupation. Cat followed her footsteps, weaving in and out between her feet. She rolled the barrel of the gun from his chest and upward to his chin, parking it. "We should toss you overboard," she seethed.

She'd reached her breaking point. My mind spun backwards to the evening the apocalypse began and I snuck out of the van with the big gun and shot Jack. Sarah was in the same spot now. I drew in a long sigh, as I had to be the voice of reason. As much as I agreed with tossing him overboard, we couldn't. He was a living being. "Put the gun down, Sarah. Two wrongs don't make a right." *Holy flippinoli I sounded like my dad!*

For a breathless minute, we watched. She shifted the piece in the back, blocking it from firing upward. The click rang through the silence. My heart pattered against my chest and I imagined his brains coating the wall behind him. "Sarah, you can't do this," my words cut through the silence.

The man's eyes were wide. The sweat from his forehead ran across his cheeks, dropping onto his chest and soaking into his cat-clawed shirt. He lifted his arms, displaying large, round armpit stains. His lips twitched against the metal of the gun's barrel.

"Give me a reason I shouldn't shoot you?" Sarah shoved the barrel into his mouth. The maniacal tone in her voice sliced through the cabin.

The man's eyes rolled into his head while his body convulsed and slunk against the wall, dropping in a puddle to the floor. Sarah gasped as if reality finally sunk in that she'd snapped. "Oh my..." She dropped the gun to her side and gawked downward at the man.

Heather rushed to her side. "He's having a seizure," she said, while taking the gun from Sarah and handing it in my direction. Me, the girl who was bad with guns, great with an ax. I snatched it from her and passed it to my dad while Heather tended to the man who was no longer shaking and convulsing but slumped against the wall, his legs spread out on the floor.

"He's burning up with fever. What kind of meds do we still have?" she asked in haste, crouched over the unconscious man. His head drooped against his shoulder.

Meds: I couldn't read any of the labels from the stuff I grabbed in Spain. "I'll check." I took a couple steps then stopped in front of my mom who still stood in the doorway, her mouth agape. "Where are they, Mom?"

As if waking from a dream she blinked her eyes. "What, honey?"

"Medicines, Mom. Where are they?"

Instead of answering she turned on her heel and headed through the yacht hall, then into the closest bathroom and opened a cabinet door revealing a built-in medicine chest filled to the brim with the bottles I'd taken in Spain.

I grabbed bottles and handed them to my mom. She gathered the bottles in her arms. I then pulled out my shirt like a bowl and dumped the rest into it. Shuffling in the hallway grabbed my attention. I shifted my gaze past my mother who stood in the doorway. My dad walked past, his hands clutched onto the man's arms, followed by Heather who clutched the man's legs.

We followed them into an empty bedroom where they laid him on the bed. As soon as the man hit the mattress Heather ripped his shirt the rest of the way and pried it off, rolling him onto one side.

My father tugged his shoes off, followed by his pants. Heather studied his nearly naked body. "Let's roll him over," she ordered and together they gently rolled him to his stomach, keeping his head to the side.

Her eyes narrowed. "There's the culprit," Heather said in little more than a whisper.

I scooted past my mother, still holding my shirt bowl filled with medicine bottles. I gasped when I saw it. A wound puffed out, red and swollen. Yellow

14

gush oozed out of it like rotten vanilla pudding. Even through the crust and puss there were distinct toothmarks. *Yuck!* I dropped the meds. The bottles clanked on the floor as they hit.

Heather sifted through them as she asked, "Do we have gauze, tape, any creams?" She shifted her eyes from the bottles towards me.

I cringed, then eyed my mother. Her eyes glued to the man's wound, her face pale as she teetered on her legs. "Mom?"

She wobbled forward. "I think I should sit."

I lifted my arm to wrap it around her shoulder but my father stopped me. "I've got her. She's always had a queasy stomach. Heather needs your help." He folded an arm around her and walked her down the hall. I assumed to the bedroom they'd chosen.

My mom hadn't seen much of the killing. She'd stayed on the boat in Spain and Italy. In Morocco she stayed in the cabin. The bite was vulgar. It was nearly as gross as the deaders; nearly, but not quite. They took the cake on disgustingness. My father in his illness didn't have any oozing wounds. He was pale and ashen but not revolting like this man's blistering, seeping bite.

"Get as many of these as you can find, stat," Heather's voice carried me back to the room and the man on the bed.

Sarah took a list from Heather and scurried past me into the hall in search of items to save the man she'd only moments ago held a gun to. I hurried to catch up with her. Matching her pace, I walked in step. "What's on the list?"

After studying it I ripped the bottom half and handed it back to her. "I got these."

She nodded, tears in her eyes. I knew Sarah, and guilt was eating at her. "I felt that moment too, Sarah, at the pier in Jacksonville when I shot Jack. It's OK." I folded her into my arms for a quick hug.

She swallowed while returning my hug then stepped back. "We need to hurry."

Chapter Three

Bennet knew the boat better than any of us so I started with him. I found him below deck, outside the engine room, slumped on his butt. A rope wound tight hung above him from a hook on the wall. It was a lucky guess for me since I knew he hid there when the soldiers came. I let out a sigh and narrowed my eyes to Bennet. "Why didn't you warn us?"

He gulped. "I, umm... I didn't know what else to do. He held the gun to me and made me do it. He threatened me!" His words spilled in a shaky voice. His hands folded as he squeezed tight around his legs.

He wasn't getting off the hook that easy. "We offered for you to come with us and there were plenty of boats docked. We could have taken another. Now we have a gun-happy maniac who's been bitten on board and we have to make a stop in another country! You're slowing down our progress!"

"I was scared. I didn't know what to do," he countered.

We didn't have time for this, I'd grill him later. "You know this yacht. It's your family's," I took a guess but when his brows formed a V and a gasp escaped his mouth I knew I'd hit the clown on his big red nose. "Get up." I held out a hand and he placed a warm palm in mine. "We have stuff to collect so maybe we can save this man's life."

At the moment I was more curious about the man's intentions and digging information out of him than I was about saving his life because he was a living being. If we didn't do something soon he'd be a zombie, I'd be axing off his head in a compassion killing and we wouldn't get anything out of him. I grabbed the rope off the wall above Bennet and we left the engine compartment.

There wasn't any tubing on board but there were a couple bags of plastic bendy straws in the kitchen, a needle point kit and syringes in one of the bedrooms as his mom had been a needle-pointing hobbyist and diabetic. I thought about the kid. He was given a sour hand like the rest of us but, unlike me, he didn't have parents or family. *Maybe I should give him a break?*

I glanced at Bennet as he sheepishly strode in step with me. His head shifted downward towards his feet in defeat or cowardice or shame, possibly all three. "I got these." My words lacked sympathy as I left him standing in the room he'd chosen as his own -- his parents'.

By the time I returned to Heather, Sarah was already there playing nurse to our Dr. Heather, handing her supplies as they treated the bite and Cat's scratches externally. I placed the items in my hand on the built-in dresser top next to Heather.

She eyed the objects and the rope in my hand. Within minutes, Sarah and I fitted the straws together and Heather crushed antibiotics into a fine powder, mixed them with water in a baggie and had a crude but effective intravenous system pumping the drugs into him.

Since he was feverish with a 104 degree temp instead of lowered body temperature and a steady normal heart beat, Heather diagnosed him as suffering from the infection caused from the bite. Of course the bite was something of a worry since it appeared human in shape but without the same symptoms my father had and Sarah hadn't suffered any when she got bit. Heather didn't think the man was turning.

I wasn't as convinced and took to the side of playing it safe. That's where the rope came in. I tied his legs together at the ankles and gathered the rope around his wrists after pulling his arms across his back. He'd be a bit uncomfy when he awoke. If he was a deader by the time that happened he would be hard pressed to eat us.

"Is that necessary?" Heather asked with a hand on the baggie as she pumped it. The mixture of medicine and water flowing into his system.

"Yes," Sarah and I answered in unison.

Heather cocked her lips to the side. "Fine. I won't argue, but he's not turning and will be awake once the antibiotics have circulated through his system."

I tightened the last knot around his wrist then ran the rope across the bed and tied it to a lamp sconce. Everything on the yacht was built in and stationary. The lamp was solid and fixed to the wall. He wasn't going anywhere. "He'll have to be upset for a hot minute."

Heather sighed her disapproval as she continued pumping the bag.

Cat scampered into the room. His back arched as he jumped sideways, fur standing on end. He growled as he leaped backwards, hitting the wall after he almost landed on the man's pants. I chuckled, "Cat doesn't like him either."

Animals had a sixth sense right? I always thought they did. In the normal world, they were known to act strangely before and during hurricanes, earthquakes, and other natural disasters and some even saved their owners' lives in tight situations.

I leaned over and stuffed my hand into the man's front pants pocket and pulled out a tiny thumb drive. I held it in my fingers then shoved it in my pocket. Sarah and Heather's eyes were glued to me. His back pocket held an ID card but it wasn't his picture on it. His other pocket had a wallet, clearly his as the driver's ID matched. I read it out loud, "His name is Eshe, he's..." I counted the years on my fingers, born in October of 1983, "almost thirty five."

There were no other pictures in his wallet or anything that suggested he had a family or what his occupation was. It didn't matter. If he had family they were probably deaders now and whatever his job was didn't exist in the new post-deader world.

"Sarah, will you continue pumping this into him? He's obviously not going anywhere since the two of you bound him into that horrible position." I heard the annoyance in her voice. At first I hadn't liked her only because Bryce couldn't take his eyes off her.

She was gorgeous, model gorgeous, but I'd grown to love her scientific, professional doctor savvy and she wasn't prissy as I originally thought.

Sarah took Heather's spot and she showed her what to do, leaving her with a radio and orders to call her if there was any change, then walked with me as I pushed towards the living area in search of Bennet.

Heather caught my arm in the hall and gave me the same firm eyes my parents did when I was in trouble.

"I don't want a lecture about tying him up. Maybe the fever and infection is masking that he's turning into a deader," I pronounced before she could get a word out.

Her brows furrowed. "Maddie, you did the right thing. The fever and infection can be masking the signs that he's turning. I don't want to panic Sarah and everyone else on board. We have to protect ourselves first. I'm not condemning you. I saw the thumb drive you quickly stuffed in your pocket but I don't think Sarah caught it. We'll take a look together, maybe there're some answers or maybe there's nothing."

Her words made sense but I didn't think painting the truth a color other than the truth was an answer, but wasn't that what doctors did? *Isn't that what the news and other adults in charge did?* Applying that logic someone, somewhere in the world knew the apocalypse was coming and hid it from the public. Red hot anger boiled in my gut then softened when my mind changed gears to the premonition Bryce and I shared, then boiled again. People don't have shared dreams and don't take objects out of dreams. *Who did this? Was the entire thing planned? And why would anyone want to kill masses of people?*

My mind couldn't grasp what it was thinking. Nobody would purposely plan a zombie apocalypse. It had to be an accident, a lab experiment gone wrong. Yet it affected people across the globe which made it planned mass killing on a scale never seen. *No, no it wasn't. It couldn't be.*

"I know where there's a computer," Heather's words interrupted my morbid thoughts, cutting them off before I imagined a malevolent scientist wringing his hands while he released a deadly virus into the atmosphere.

"That beats my idea of threatening Bennet," I responded without emotion.

She sucked in a breath. "Bennet is a scared child."

"So was I before I started slashing deaders," I mumbled under my breath.

I knew she heard me but didn't respond. I was glad she said nothing because I was still just a kid, no more than a couple years older than Bennet. My innocent, normal teenage life was over forever. We neared the galley and the thick aroma of food hit my nostrils. My stomach instantly grumbled as I hadn't eaten in a while.

"In here," Heather whispered as she cut sharp to the left and visions of devouring food poofed from my head like magic fairy dust.

The room housed a sleek black table with plush benches on either side. She dropped onto one, pulled a drawer from beneath the table and lifted a small laptop out of it. I took the seat next to her and refrained from asking how she knew this was here. It might have been a lucky guess, as this room resembled an office of types with built in bookcases. They weren't loaded down heavy with books but had a few hardbacks and knickknacks behind the black bar that ran across each shelf.

The computer booted up and I stuck the drive in the USB port. It wasn't password protected so we got right in and went to the drive which *was* password protected. *Darn, nothing could be easy in this insane world.*

We spent the next several minutes discussing the commonalities between every country we'd been through. The only things they all had in common were zombies and survivors. Defeat rippled through me. There had to be something else.

Determination painted across Heather's face as she racked her brain. "You're a smart girl, Maddie. We can do this." Her words gave me some comfort but the longer this took for us to figure it out the less chance we had and we needed in.

My trust in Eshe, the possibly infected man, was slimmer than a string. I wanted him to live and not turn so I could grill him. *What did he know? What's on the drive?* I figured since it was in his possession then, logically, he knew something.

Heather's face lit up and she cupped her cheeks. "Those bugs. The little black ones. What are they again?"

"Lovebugs," I responded, at first unsure where she was going, then it hit me. They were everywhere. Native to Florida or South America they were invasive in Italy, Morocco, and Spain.

"Try it," she urged.

I typed 'lovebugs' into the box and no luck. Passwords couldn't be that simple and probably needed a number so I typed in 'l0vebug5' and still no luck.

"There needs to be a capital," Heather offered, leaning close to the screen as if that would make the combination work.

I punched in 'L0vebug5' and no luck. Tapping my fingers against my legs, my mind deep in thought, I remembered the ID I found that wasn't Eshe's. I pulled it out of my pocket. It had a South African address on it. The man in the picture was white with wisps of brown hair combed over his shining, balding head. He looked like a scientist with thick coke bottle glasses and a lab coat. I was stereotyping. Shrugging my shoulders; I didn't care. His name was Oliver Davies. A logo with a green tree surrounded by a blue circle and the letters WEAC.

We-yak. I knew what that stood for. The company Bryce's father was working with -- Wetland Environment and Conservation. *There was a branch in South Africa? How big was this company and how deep in the zombie apocalypse were they?*

I handed Heather the card. She eyed it then glanced at me. "Isn't that the same company Bryce's father works for or with?"

I nodded, then tried variations of WEAC and the man's name, but no luck. I leaned my head backwards and blew out a long breath, ready to give up.

I heard Heather type something into the cryptic box. "We're in!"

"What?" I realized I said it out loud when Heather glanced at me.

"I got it. Why would he use his name or the company name? A good password has a capital letter, lowercase letters, a number and a character. I always hated trying to remember so many combinations to log into the bank, at work, paying my bills." She pushed a wave of hair that came loose from the ponytail behind her ear. "My point is to use a password that has meaning and will be easily remembered, so if this is his and work related it makes sense to use the project name so I tried '10ve_Bug5'."

The radio crackled from its spot on the table top and Sarah's voice beamed through.

Chapter Four

Jack and Bryce

Bryce made it to the engine room. The sound grew louder as he moved each level lower. Sucking in a deep breath he caught a whiff of rotting flesh smell. No doubt a deader was in the room. He released his breath and twisted the knob then pushed with his shovel to keep distance between him and whatever was in the room.

The door wide open, he saw nothing. It wasn't a large area, with few places to hide, at least for an average-sized adult or even a teenager. With his shovel low, he swept the compartment. Jack's hefty footsteps on the stairs outside the door drew closer. "In here," called Bryce. "Be careful."

The door creaked open and Jack entered. Bryce didn't turn around but kept his shovel low as he continued to follow the scratching sound. Something caught his shoe. He glanced down and a rat was attached to it, attempting to nibble through his leather sneaker. He was glad he wasn't wearing flops. Instead of squashing it with his shovel, as that would prove to injure his foot too, he kicked his leg. The rat flung hard against the metal wall and dropped.

"What the heck is that?" Jack yelled as if they weren't in the small confines of the engine room. His voice echoed off the walls and the rat scampered forward and jumped at him. The one thing zombies had in common, besides being not quite alive, was they reacted to noise. Its little claws clung to his jeans and its mouth opened wide, displaying its sharp teeth.

Jack thrust the barrel of his rifle between his leg and the rat in time so that its teeth clashed against the metal and he shoved it off. The little monster went flying and Bryce, using knee jerk reaction time, caught it in the blade of his shovel but it dropped quicker than he could swat it to the floor and trap it. The little creature scurried around the room, disoriented.

Bryce swatted at it, hitting the ground with a large bang that hurt his ears, but it managed to escape and scampered beneath engine equipment.

"Let's trap this thing," suggested Jack as he moved towards the door. Bryce followed, their eyes searching for the rat so it wouldn't follow them out.

Once the door swung shut Jack said, "I have an idea. That little rat zombie wants us for a meal. Well, that just ain't going to happen. There're some fishing poles I spotted earlier. I say we catch us something and serve it alive and wriggling."

It was a brilliant plan and Bryce was a great fisherman. The only problem was going to be bait. He doubted there was anything alive on the boat they could use.

Jack returned to the bridge and coasted the yacht out of the ship's wake. Traveling in it with his trained eye and boating skills was dangerous enough, but the consequences could be dire if he didn't slow it down a bit. Their speed would also make fishing a difficult process.

Bryce searched high and low and came up with canned meat but hated to use that as they needed it more for sustenance. Not knowing what started the zombie outbreak, and what living things were infected, they didn't trust eating animals. It had done them well so far, as everyone in the group was still on the living side of life and not the deader side.

Bryce found a bag of gummy bears in the cabinet. It was already opened and they were a bit tough. "What do you think? We can soak them for a couple minutes and soften them up."

Jack scratched his bald head. "That's genius. I've heard tales candy works well as fish bait."

Bryce had never heard that, but he didn't have Jack's Coast Guard background. He was sure he'd heard all sorts of tales and myths.

Within a few minutes they readied two poles and stood at the stern. Deep sea fishing wasn't new to Bryce but this was the first time he'd tried it this far off the coast and never on a yacht this size that was in motion. However, he knew enough to understand their best chance of catching something was from the stern. After nearly an hour of waiting, something tugged at Jack's pole. He began reeling it in. "Got something."

Bryce propped his pole and joined Jack who was struggling with his catch. Together they worked to reel it in, then the line went slack and Jack fell over. The line on the fishing pole thrust over their heads, landing with a ping on the deck.

Jack scrambled to his feet and followed Bryce. They ran over to inspect it and stared in dismay when they noted just a fish head. Its body was chomped clean off.

"That's no good," said Bryce as he scooped the head onto his shovel.

"It's not moving, least it was alive," noted Jack, pleased it wasn't a zombie fish. He didn't know if the little zombie rat preferred living meat or dead meat but figured living would be best.

Bryce flipped it into the water. It landed with a splash, then he rushed towards his pole as he spotted his line pulling away from the boat. Reeling it in the way his father taught him, within a few minutes a full fish, a tuna he thought, crested the water. He continued pulling the line in when out of the water rose a pointed nose and sharp teeth, followed by a rotten scent, aimed for his fish.

"No, you're not, Sharknado wanna be!" he screamed at it as he flung the pole over his head. The tuna hit the deck with a thud. The shark dropped back into the water. "Did you see that?"

Jack's face twisted in obvious confusion. "That shark. It was... it was a zombie shark?"

Bryce nodded. Its smell gave away its level of life, same as the rat. Most fish stunk but the smell of zombies was something worse and far more potent. They scurried around the boat to the fish. Its gills moving in and out rapidly. It was still alive, not dead alive. He scooped it up and dumped it in the bucket of water they had waiting, then carried it below deck.

Jack followed him and carefully eased open the engine room door as they slid the bucket with the fish inside. Letting the door drop back into place but not completely closed, as they'd left it open a slit in order to catch the rat. They'd trap it in the bucket.

Through the sliver between the door and frame, one of Bryce's eyes peered into the room as the zombie rat ran towards the bucket and took the bait. He clutched the bucket lid in his hand, ready to squash it on top.

Chapter Five

Maddie

Eshe still hadn't woken but Sarah successfully pumped the contents of the baggie into the man's arm. Since it was hooked to his vein I wasn't sure why Heather had Sarah pump it but figured maybe it was a sneaky doctor thing again and she didn't want anyone knowing about the thumb drive yet. She did mention she didn't think Sarah saw me slip it into my pocket.

I swallowed a bite of Vienna sausages smothered in garlic-flavored white rice. It was pretty amazing what my mom could do with canned and boxed foods. I quickly scooped another bite into my mouth.

"Are you hungry?" asked my mom in a mocking yet friendly tone.

It wasn't simply that I was starving, which I was, but I wanted to get back to the thumb drive. We hadn't had the chance to snoop through its contents before Sarah radioed, followed almost immediately by my mom announcing dinner was ready.

I smiled, then changed the subject. Glancing at my father who slipped a steaming bite into his mouth, I asked, "Are we still headed to Cape Town?" Now, with the drive and since finding that ID in Eshe's pocket, Cape Town seemed like a good idea.

He swallowed and without any suspicion in his voice said, "Yes, I know it's out of the way but if he wakes I think we owe it to him and his family. I couldn't imagine how I'd feel knowing my family was trapped somewhere without me. He didn't mean what he did earlier. He was scared and he's ill."

He said that as the father he is. Man to man. He had a soft heart and might have done something just as crazy to save his own family. "I was thinking that too," I agreed for good measure.

My mom scowled. "What if he doesn't make it? Then we've wasted gas and time."

Heather piped in, "We can refuel there, even stock up on food. I think we should."

Katrina seconded the idea and it was set. We were on our way to Cape Town.

A groan echoed through the hall filtering into the dining area. That meant one of two things, Eshe was either awake and in pain or still out and moaning in his sleep. Either way he was alive, but alive as in living or alive as in dead-alive I didn't know. The deaders moaned and groaned.

Heather scooted off her chair, wiped her mouth, set the napkin on the table and excused herself. She was so proper even at a time like this. Two steps from the table, Cat flew past her, jumping high into the air and landing on all fours in a pounce position. The hair on his back prickled like a cactus. That couldn't be good. My heart thumped like a drummer on an energy drink in my chest.

Heather paused for a second to avoid being hit by Cat in the shoulder then glanced at him in his resting spot, shrugged, and continued down the hall.

Sarah chuckled, then her lips drew into a straight line and her chuckles stopped cold. "He's been acting weird like when..." She paused, glanced at my father and swallowed hard. "You woke up after fighting off the zombie sickness."

Her words lingered in the air for a few silent seconds before my father wiped his face and set the napkin on the table beside his bowl. "We shouldn't worry based on Cat's actions. His life has been turned upside down too, and I'm fine."

The old wives' tale said animals sensed things. *What did Cat sense?* My dad got through it, maybe Eshe would too. At this point, I hoped he would. I didn't feel like compassion killing anyone. The yacht gave the illusion of peace.

I literally shoveled down the last few bites in my bowl and excused myself. I wasn't about to waste food. My mind battled with itself. *Do I go back to the drive or help Heather?* I really didn't want to help. My curiosity about the contents of the drive was making me crazy. Sarah excused herself at the same time and made it to the hallway before me since her seat was closer. She was going to help Heather so I could get back to the drive.

Without another thought, I beelined to the office and computer. I stared aghast at the contents of the drive and a letter to the British Parliament. More curious than its contents is why Eshe had it on his person. He wasn't a member of parliament since his license was South African. *Was he a courier?* If so, why would they choose to send this information via carrier instead of encrypted email or something where it would reach its intended viewers much quicker?

The letter explained individual zombie incidences encountered in the U.S. Specifically Florida. The first was two years ago in Jacksonville but they were spreading at an alarming rate and moving into other states; Georgia, Louisiana, and Mississippi to name a few. The government cleaned up the mess but didn't put a halt to the mosquito testing that led to the deadly lovebugs.

Lovebugs! I knew it! They were an experiment that went horribly wrong, I thought, but still had no actual proof of that. I leaned in, my eyes glued to the screen as I continued to read. When a lovebug was hit by a car it splattered like all bugs except, in its splatter, it released acid. That acid was responsible for releasing something into the air that caused people to become ill and take on characteristics of a dead person. Their heart continued to beat slowly, lowering their pulse rate, and their chest and lungs continued to take in oxygen, send out carbon dioxide, and their brains continued only minimal function.

Lovebugs and mosquitos? Bryce's father was an environmental scientist working in water management and claimed lovebugs didn't really eat mosquitoes, so how did a chemical agent aimed for decreasing the mosquito population end up inside lovebugs, making people sick? It seemed the mosquitoes should make us sick since they were carrying the virus or whatever.

There were graphs and charts documenting all incidences of infection at the time this disk was created. There was also documentation of sick individuals found in South Africa. They held them for testing instead of putting them out of their misery. The facility was located in Cape Town.

Cape Town: that's why Eshe was determined enough to hold us at gunpoint. I pulled out the ID tag I found. A strand of loose hair fell over it. I blew it away and stared at the picture. He was a scientist. Putting two and two together, he worked at the lab in Cape Town. *How did Eshe fit into all this?*

Was he a carrier? Were they traveling together? Carrying documentation to Britain in hopes of gaining help and halting the spread of the illness so it didn't erupt into a worldwide epidemic. They were too late and the drive lacked any information on how to stop it or a cure.

Were world leaders and scientists all meeting in Britain with hopes of putting their heads together and stopping this thing? I didn't know, but the contents of this disk were proof the world leaders knew and kept this from people everywhere.

I blinked rapidly as it all sunk into my mind and lovebugs fluttered behind my eyelids. *Lovebugs mate twice yearly. Every spring and every fall. It only lasts a couple weeks, tops. What happens in the fall when the new ones are born? Will the disease mutate and kill the rest of us?*

Footsteps in the hall alerted me someone was close by, possibly on their way into the study. I closed the document and pulled the thumb drive from the computer, stuffing it back into my pocket.

My father's head peeked around the door, his blue eyes vibrant and blazing into mine.

"Hi, Dad," I said as nonchalant as possible.

"What do you have there?" he asked as he took a seat next to me.

"Just a computer. I thought maybe the owners might have some good music or something on it."

He lowered his brows. "Or pictures, something to help you remember life before it changed?"

That thought hadn't hit me but, in this situation, I agreed. A little white lie wouldn't harm anything. "Life has gotten crazy. I've forgotten what it used to be like."

"Me too." He reached for the computer. "Do you mind?"

I pushed it towards him. "Not at all. We'll look together."

He opened some files and we looked at pictures of people we didn't know, except for Bennet dressed in normal looking clothes. It wasn't like we could go online or to the mall and shop so we wore what we found that fit and Bennet found strange combinations like plaids and stripes, baggy clothes with tight clothes. He hadn't looked as bad again as the day we met him but still wasn't fashionable.

Sarah bounced into the study, her dark curls springing with each step. Heather followed behind her. Sarah dropped onto the bench next to me. Her eyes immediately fixed to the photos.

Heather leaned against the doorframe. "He's still asleep and very much alive. I gave him more sedatives and pumped another dose of antibiotics into him."

My dad kissed the top of my head and joined Heather. They strolled out the door. Their muffled voices carried into the room as they talked.

"They were so happy," Sarah sighed as she gazed at the pictures of Bennet and his family.

Weren't we all, I thought, but didn't say anything as her mother was one of the first to go when the infection hit. All the puzzle pieces were falling into place. My father, Bryce's father, Sarah's mother were all in car wrecks when they were exposed to the sickness. It was lovebug season. The nasty creatures smashed against the grills of the cars, their acid went airborne carrying the illness. That's how they were infected!

"How long has it been do you think?" Sarah asked in a quiet, thoughtful voice, her head leaned against my shoulder.

How long has it been? I didn't really know. "Maybe a couple months?" I answered, more as a question than a statement.

She pulled her head up. "I don't think so. It took us eleven days to get to Spain then another couple days to get to Italy and we spent a couple weeks in Morocco, so by my calculations it's only been about a month."

That was it? It seemed like so much longer like a millennia. We'd have to rewrite the history books after building a new civilization but that was a lifetime away.

"You want to do something normal?" she asked, her lips curled in a wide smile.

What was normal? I scanned the room and it gave an illusion; soft, puffy benches, sleek black furnishings and a built in big screen TV. "Yeah, I do. What are you thinking?"

She turned to me. "I saw popcorn, the microwave kind, when I was helping put stuff away and there're movies." She pointed to the shelf.

I hadn't even noticed the collection. We locked gazes then jumped off the bench together and ran towards the DVD collection. They were all mainstream U.S. movies. *Titanic, Zombieland* -- we glanced at each other and cringed. In the old days, heck yeah, we would have watched it, but not in this world.

Sarah scattered the DVDs across the floor. "*Pitch Perfect!*" she screamed.

It was one of our favorites. Within minutes we were sneaking into the kitchen and stuffing a bag of popcorn in the microwave. Everyone else was below deck in the living room area which meant we were alone with a possible zombie turning man only feet away from us. *Oh well, I had him tied up tight!*

We stuffed *Pitch Perfect* into the DVD player and fluffed a few pillows onto the floor then placed the bag of popcorn between us. The aroma of warm butter melted into my nostrils and I shoved a handful into my mouth.

Two movies later, my eyelids heavy like lead, I fell asleep and awoke when eerie noises squeaked and moaned like Earnest Earl during the tsunami that ripped him apart. The moon gave the only light that shone from the hallway. I called for Sarah but she didn't answer. *Where is she?* Dread slunk into my gut. The uneasy feeling that soon I'd be surrounded by deaders.

I rose and did a quick search for any weapon, the empty bag of popcorn and pillows wouldn't do much to kill a deader. *Where is everyone?* The books, DVDs and computer wouldn't be effective weapons either. Remembering Heather pulled the computer from a drawer below the table, I scurried to it and yanked it open. I rummaged through the pens and papers in the drawer. A pen up the nostril or through the eye socket might do something but I'd have to get real close. With a twist of my mouth and the vision of a pencil stuck into the eye of a deader I dug further into the drawer. A flashlight. It was heavy enough that if I clunked them on the head hard it might do some good.

I stalked towards the hall and sniffed. There was no telltale rancid odor of deaders. With that in mind I plastered my back against the wall and slid towards the kitchen. From a drawer I pulled out a large, sharp knife and held it in front of me. It would do far more than a heavy flashlight.

The rattle of chains grabbed my attention then stopped. I froze and listened for several seconds for the sound but didn't hear it again until I took a step away from the drawer. It sounded as if it was coming from the lower level. Standing on the precipice of the steps, the rattle sounded again, closer. Loud, long scrapes crescendoed through my ears, dragging across the tile of the kitchen, made my breath catch. I slid along the wall, my feet on the first step, my head peeking around the corner.

A bulky shadow limped from the hallway. The chains dragging from its wrists. I sucked in a breath as it stopped in front of the window, bathed in moonlight. I sucked in another deep breath. The air was clean and fresh. The gut wrenching odor of rot absent. Deaders stunk. I studied the man. Even with its shoulders hunched I recognized him. *Eshe! How did he get out?*

My mind processed what my eyes were seeing. It couldn't be. *I didn't use a chain but ropes and where was everyone?* I blinked several times. He lifted his head and opened his mouth. A long pained groan escaped his lips and his eyes stared blankly at me. There was nothing in them -- dead eyes. He picked up a foot then another and *drip dragged* towards me.

The cool metal handle of the knife in my hand, I stepped out of my hiding spot. One slow painful step at a time he drifted towards me but something was wrong. Zombies didn't see, they smelled like rotten trash and they didn't make calculated decisions, yet this man was headed for me. His mouth opened wide, a line of drool fell over his chin.

I threw the flashlight across the room. His eyes didn't leave mine and he didn't acknowledge the clunk it made when it hit the floor. My mind raced in confusion, all the mental notes I'd taken on zombies from the very beginning I'd have to rewrite. *Were they evolving?* Impossible in only a few weeks.

"Maddie," Eshe called in a much higher tone than he used earlier. Drool continued to roll over his chin. "Maddie." His mouth was moving but it couldn't be him. It couldn't. There was someone else on the boat. I tried to place the voice. It wasn't Sarah or my mom, Heather or Katrina, and certainly not little Melissa.

I turned on my heel and rushed down the steps. My hand wrapped around the handle of the knife, I flew through the space, opening each door to find emptiness and loneliness. Something brushed against my shoulder. In complete Zombie Girl mode I whipped around, Eshe's mouth dropped to my face, mouth opened wide, drool puddling over my cheeks. Before I could plunge the knife into him, his teeth sunk into my cheek.

"Maddie, Maddie," cut through the fog and two brown eyes inside a dark face stared at me. I was no longer in the lower level of the yacht and Bennet was staring at me. The TV was black as it had instantly shut off after the movie ended and Sarah lay beside me on the pillow, snoring gently.

Chapter Six

I scrambled to my feet and pushed past Bennet then raced to Eshe's room. Footsteps pattering against the floor told me Bennet was following. When I got to the room, Eshe's awkwardly tied form was visible through the moonlight. I stalked into the room and around the bed searching for his face.

"He's asleep," came Bennet's voice in a reassuring tone. The kindness of it gave me a huge guilt trip. I'd been onto the boy, mean, strict, and jumped all over him. He didn't deserve that. Bennet was a scared kid. His velvet brown eyes spoke in innocence and confusion lines wrinkled his forehead.

I had to see for myself. When I found the man's face I stared into his closed eyes. Soft flesh and dark long eyelashes didn't flutter. I poked him and, again, nothing. He was asleep and the dream was trying to tell me something, something on the edge of my brain.

The thing that made everyone ill was released when the lovebugs blew up. The thing was one of those science words I always forgot; para... anti... pathogen! Contagious illnesses were caused by pathogens such as bacteria, fungus, and viruses. My head was now reciting the science lesson. An organism that carried the pathogen and made other organisms sick was a vector like lovebugs. Their acid and the wind carried it to parts unknown. To have spread so quickly and so far, I determined it had a long shelf life. We had to find a way to stop them. To reverse the effects.

"I don't think he's a zombie," Bennet walked up beside me. Together we stared at the sleeping man.

I thought about that. He didn't have similar symptoms to my father, but that was different as my dad was exposed directly to the airborne pathogen after the car accident and probably Bryce's father too since he was also in a car wreck before falling ill. If the pathogen was airborne, did it spread through bodily fluids like in the movies? "Why don't you think he's a zombie?" That was the better question.

"Because my parents got sick right away, so did everyone else. But he doesn't look like a zombie or smell like one." Wise words from a young man.

He was right. The bite was extra disgusting and infected but his temperature, heart rate, and breathing were normal. My dad bit Sarah and she never had a symptom. Heather gave her antiviral medication, but the bite was a day or two old before we got to Sarah. No, Eshe wasn't turning into a zombie. The pathogen was airborne, not transferred through body fluids. I loosened the ropes holding Eshe. He should at least be comfortable when he awoke.

"I think you're right. This illness passes through the air not body fluids." It was time for a group meeting. With that thought, I had Bennet help me wake everyone and meet below in the lounge area.

Within twenty minutes the groggy-eyed group of adults and Sarah glared at me. I bit my lip.

"Get on with it, Maddie," Heather spoke, pushing long dark curls out of her face and pushing them behind her ears.

This was it. I swallowed. "Um, I think the pathogen that causes people to become deaders is airborne and not passed from body fluids. Think about it. Sarah didn't get ill, no symptoms at all, but Dad," I glanced his way for a split second, "and Bryce's father were exposed directly through the air after their car accidents. The lovebugs splattered and it was released through their acids. Dad is fine. We don't," I paused for a second, "know about Bryce's father."

Heather cleared her throat. "We know it's airborne but why do you think it doesn't pass through bodily fluids?"

"All the people we've seen with bites covering their bodies we don't know if that's what made them sick. Right, they could have gotten sick when the acid released the pathogen," I was proud of my correct science vocab, "and then, because they work on basic minimal functions, tried eating each other."

Katrina grimaced as if memories of the nasty things crossed her mind. I thought their smell was worse than their appearance.

My dad scratched his head. "How do you know the pathogen is released in the acid of lovebugs?"

Uh oh. My lips pulled into a cheesy smile and I glanced at Heather. She narrowed her eyes and glared back. The cat was out of the bag and I was giving her the lead. She was the doctor, after all.

Illness was her thing, not mine. I was simply the biology amateur.

She straightened her back and told them about the flash drive I found and its contents. When she was finished everyone stared at her in disbelief as if we had kept the end of the world secret from them; but we hadn't, only a few details about how it started.

My mom broke the silence, her eyes roving between Heather and I, "When were you planning on sharing this?"

"Um..." I was quickly interrupted by Heather.

"We only just learned this today and wanted to check out the facility first."

My mom stood, fire in her eyes. "You are concerned about that lab. You lied. It was never about that man's family. He lied too. I don't believe he has family there. We shouldn't stop. It's not worth the risk. You want to get to a science lab infested with this zombie sickness!"

Or whatever, or whatever... "We don't know what we're going to find there and, if nothing else, there will be equipment we can bring onboard the yacht. The trip to Jacksonville will give Heather time to research the illness and how it affects us. We need to combat it before the next wave of lovebugs in the fall." I reminded everyone of that. This wasn't a freak one-time thing. The lovebugs were twice yearly.

Calm and collected, my father responded, "This is something that should be done. We need to follow every lead so we are still making the stop in Cape

Town. We also need food so I will come with you day one and we'll gas the yacht and gather supplies." He turned to Katrina, "Please check though our medications and toiletries, make note of anything we need." He tilted his head towards my mom, "We need a list of food." He ran his hand over his scruffy chin. "In another day we'll be in Cape Town. Today we prepare."

My dad, in control. In leader mode. Probably what he was like at work and always when I was in trouble. Katrina and my mom rose. Since we were all awake it was time to get to work. Heather and I packed our weapons and food for the trip. The first day was meant as a day trip, but one never knew what terror we'd meet.

Chapter Seven

As the yacht drifted into the port of Cape Town the city spread out sheltered by mountains. It wasn't large, but crowded. Building after building crept towards the high region that appeared to reach into the sky. Dark clouds blocked most of the sun and a light drizzle trickled against my head.

Eshe was still delirious. The bite looked like dried raisins but he didn't make any sense when he spoke. In another day or two hopefully. I figured he'd come to sometime while we were here, so did my father. He promised if he didn't wake up while we were docked we wouldn't waste more time in getting to Jacksonville.

Sarah also volunteered. I didn't know why and she got the same speech and incredulous looks from my parents. It was decided with a ton of insisting and dubious looks from my father that she would be part of our "Cape Town" day one team. If it wasn't for Heather also volunteering my parents would have put up a larger fight even after their little come to reality proposition in Morocco stating that, in the current condition of the world, we were adults. I actually thought they worried more for her safety than mine, but possibly it was my imagination.

"Be careful, Maddie," my mother whispered in my ear as she folded me into her arms and held me tight like a favorite teddy bear. It wasn't like I wouldn't see her again.

My father gassed the yacht up quickly and we coasted it far enough from the port that a zombie couldn't board. If it tried, it would drop like lead into the ocean. After lowering the anchor Heather, Sarah, my father, and I boarded the life boat and rowed to port. It was empty, as we'd noted when gassing the yacht.

We tied the tiny boat as it bounced gently on the water and one by one stepped onto the platform. It was as deathly silent as everywhere else. The one thing I had never gotten used to. We had no idea how close we'd find supplies and how many deaders awaited us. The clouds in the sky burned off and the sun baked the tops of our heads.

Cape Town was a large city in a small space. The roads were littered with stopped cars and dead bodies. Really dead bodies. Bullets in many of their heads. There were still living people here. It had not been cleansed as we called it. *But where were the living and the dead?*

That question was partially answered when we stumbled upon a row of shops. Through the glass, deaders pawed and moaned. Their dead eyes didn't follow or watch us and I figured they didn't see us and through the glass probably didn't smell us either.

"How are we going to do this?" Sarah asked as we all stared into the store's window and the large group milling about.

"I think we find another store," suggested Heather. "We don't know enough about this illness and how it spreads to want any food from this one."

I didn't see where that would matter; canned goods were sealed, so were water bottles, and even boxed foods.

I suggested this, but Heather cringed. "There is a whole city."

My dad nodded in agreement. "There're too many inside. There'll be another grocery."

A couple blocks over, more dead bodies strewn over the sidewalks and in the roads. They were getting thicker, but dead. We zigzagged through them until finding another grocery. Again there were deaders inside, but not so many.

My father tapped the glass and dead snarling bodies ran towards us. I counted five. That would be a breeze. "This one?" I asked.

Heather nodded in agreement and the four of us came up with a plan. Sarah would rap on the glass of the door -- we wanted to alert them, but not every deader in the city -- then she would open it, keeping herself behind it for the bit of protection the glass allowed. My father and I would enter. It was a decent plan but not the same without Bryce -- my zombie killing buddy. Heather would shoot those we didn't decapitate. Hopefully none. Bullets fired would get too much attention in an uncleansed city. Silence was our friend.

Once the door was opened, the deaders drip dragged onto the sidewalk, catching our scent carried on the ocean breeze. I sliced through their necks while my father swung a hoe towards their heads. I told him the front or back of the neck, but his aim stunk. His went down with large gashes across their

49

faces. The top of their heads hanging at the cheek. I glared at him and slammed my ax through the necks of each of his kills to be sure they were dead.

I yanked my ax from the neck of the last one. "Dad, severing their brainstem kills them for good. It's most effective, anyways."

He smirked. "My way seemed effective too, as they didn't get back up."

I sighed. He had a point.

Inside the store we checked all the rooms. They were empty so we filled bags with food, anything that was in a sealed package, along with shampoo, toothpaste, toilet paper and laundry soap.

"There's a pharmacy across the street. We don't need anything but I think we should stock up anyway. It's always best to be prepared," Heather said as she gripped her bags.

"I'll go," I offered.

"We'll both go."

The shelves of the store were empty now. My father and Sarah stayed inside the grocery with all the bags as Heather and I scooted across the deader-free street.

We didn't spot any zombies inside the pharmacy so I tapped the window. Still none answered. "I think it's safe."

Heather nodded and she pushed the door open. A tiny bell attached to the door rang. It reminded me of walking into a neighborhood store and being greeted, but nothing greeted us here but silence. Drugs were tossed everywhere and dead deaders lay across the floor. Their heads bashed in, I knew they weren't getting up.

Everything was picked pretty clean but we found some band aids, a couple boxes of antibiotic pills and a few things still behind the counter. I couldn't read the labels but Heather grabbed them as if they were gold.

"We have enough. Let's go," she stated as we stepped onto the street, first making sure the coast was clear. We stole across the street. My eyes fixed on the store, something was different. A large form passed behind a row of shelves. My mind knew immediately that wasn't my father and was most definitely too large to be Sarah. "Stop," I whispered to Heather. "Someone else is in there."

She grabbed my arm and pulled me to the side of the store out of the view from the window. We braced ourselves along the wall. "I saw it too and I think there's a second person in there with them."

Two people? "We have to get in there." The wheels in my hamster brain were spinning.

She nodded. "Wasn't there a back door?"

When I'd checked the storeroom I was looking for deaders not doors but thought I remembered seeing one. "I think so."

"We go around back and find it." I knew she would say that. In the scary movies they always do. Unfortunately this was real life. My life.

Together, we stalked through the alley like cat burglars. A shuffling drip drag echoed through my ears but didn't sound like more than one or two deaders. Easy peasy. I peeked around the corner of

51

the alley. It wasn't what I wanted to see. Three zombies shuffled along, chunks of flesh hanging from their arms and faces. Their skin ashy and gray. None of them looked older than me. That hit home. One of them could be me if we hadn't gone to sea. *Was it the ocean that saved us?* I truly wondered if we'd just gotten lucky because we weren't near land and lovebugs.

Heather took in a deep breath. She didn't like the idea of killing three teens any more than I did but it had to be done. I ran towards the tallest one and kicked her in the back. She sailed to the ground and hit it with a thud. I then slammed my ax into the back of her neck then the next. Heather had only a handgun but used it effectively to knock one onto the ground laying the ground work for me to slam my ax into its brainstem.

It was team work and within a couple minutes all three were dead dead and we put our ears towards the back door. Not hearing anything, she pulled the door open a sliver, enough for us to sneak inside. Voices loud and clear caught our ears and we stared at each other.

One voice, deep like a man's said, "I'm sorry we have to do this but you understand. It's all about survival. We won't kill you but can't have you following us either." There was a pause then he spoke again, "Make them tighter. We don't want them getting loose until we are far away."

"They're tying them up," I whispered to Heather.

She leaned towards my ear, so close I felt her warm breath. "They're leaving. Once they're gone we can untie your dad and Sarah."

Slightly annoyed, I whispered back, "They are taking our food. We worked for those bags and slayed the zombies. They probably watched us from another store and when we left went in after us seeing we hadn't taken food bags out of the store." I wasn't going to put up with this.

As if she read my mind, Heather narrowed her eyes. "You're not playing heroine. We'll find another store."

The stockroom was dark and it gave me an idea. "No, that's our food. We need a plan."

Annoyed, Heather rolled her eyes. "What is your plan?"

"We make noise back here. They come back and we whack them on the head. There're two of them and two of us. We can do this."

Double annoyance in her voice she answered, "If you hit anyone with that ax, you'll kill them. We can't kill the living."

"Then what do you suggest?"

She placed a palm against her forehead. "I'll go in with the gun. Scare them."

It could work, but I doubted she'd use the gun and figured they'd doubt it as well. They'd see a supermodel and she'd never shoot so I'd have to find a way to rescue all three. "How about I go in with the gun?" I would shoot without hesitation, although I wasn't sure what I might hit.

"No, you're a kid and that's what they'll see."

She was so stubborn. "And you're a supermodel-doctor!" My voice was a couple notches louder than I meant it.

The stock room doors swung open and the sunlight from the front windows made the figure in the doorway dark and menacing. "What do we have here?"

Heather lifted the gun, she held it squarely in both hands. She looked like an actress playing a part. The extremely hot assassin that nobody expected.

"Let them go!" she demanded, no hesitation or waver of her hands. She was acting this part well.

I glanced from her to him and saw a glint of something in his eye. *Was he scared?* Another idea rolled into my head. To pull it off I thought back to how scared I was when we first realized the zombie apocalypse was happening. The quiver in my voice sounded real as the words spilled from my lips. "Listen to her. She's crazy. She'll shoot me, you, and anyone in the other room."

His fat cheeks pulled out and a smile lit his lips. That ticked her off. She moved forward, gun in hand. The man moved backwards through the swinging stockroom doors as if he finally realized she meant business. The smile on his face gone. His lips and brows flat. "OK, OK."

A smaller man stood behind Sarah and my father. Seeing both men in the light, neither appeared as though they'd showered since the whole thing began. They both had a bad case of greasy bedhead, sweat and bloodstains coated their clothing. I was thankful at the moment I was too far away to smell the pungent odors that no doubt were radiating off them. I imagined the green wave like in the cartoons that always meant something stinky. My thought was interrupted by a loud pop.

The large man stumbled backwards into the shelving behind him. One by one all the shelves fell like dominoes. When the clanging halted and the entire row of shelves lay on the ground a steady stream of blood raced from the man, puddling on the floor.

I turned to Heather, my mouth wide in an O, "You shot him!"

She shook her head in disbelief. "No, the gun. It fired. I didn't pull it, my finger wasn't on the trigger. I... I..." She stumbled backwards and leaned against the wall.

I wasn't going to let the moment go. Sarah and my father stared at me, horrified either from the large man going down or them being tied and gagged. Probably both. I grabbed the gun from Heather's hand and aimed it at the small man.

He lifted his hands into the air. "I'll do whatever you want. There's a van in the back. Take it and take me." He dug his hand into his pocket.

"Stop!" *Was he going for a weapon?*

"It's the keys." He pulled his hand out and opened his palm. A set of shiny silver keys were in it.

"Toss them and untie them." I was surprised how cool and collected I was on the outside, because inside I was a jumble of nerves. I didn't kill living people.

"Can I get my knife for the ropes?" he asked.

55

For extra emphasis so he didn't think to try anything heroic I stated, "I'm good with the gun and better with this." I pulled the bloody ax from my waist. I kept it tucked between my pants and belt.

He nodded. "Yes Ma'am."

I was possibly enjoying this too much. After he had the ropes and gags off a moan bounced off the walls in the small store. The large man. He wasn't dead. As the thought entered my head, Heather sprinted to his side, her mind returning from the darkness and jumping into lifesaving mode.

"He's not dead, help me!" She started assessing the damage, undoing the layers of clothes around his torso.

We joined her side. A large piece of metal stuck through his gut.

"The shot didn't kill him. When he fell he punctured his internal organs. If we remove him he'll bleed out quicker." Her eyes darted around the room. "There's nothing here. I can't save him. I can't save him." Her voice frantic.

The man opened his mouth, blood drained from his lips and he uttered something unintelligible. He mumbled again, "Sho... gurgle...t... me."

The words slow and labored, but I understood as his eyes locked on mine then shifted to the gun in my hand. I aimed it at his forehead.

"What are you doing?" Heather screamed.

"There's no chance for him. He'll die a painful death or I can compassion kill him." With that, I pulled the trigger. To my astonishment the bullet went straight between his eyes. Blood puddled from the back of his head. It was so much harder to kill a living person than a deader.

For several moments no one spoke. The room was silent and the pop from the bullet echoed inside my head until my father broke the silence, "We have to go. All the noise surely alerted the dead."

"How well do you know this city?" Sarah asked the small man with an obvious plan in her mind.

"Anywhere you need to go. But what's in it for me?"

I couldn't believe he was bargaining at a moment like this. Then again, wouldn't anyone?

"We have a yacht and will take you with us."

Chapter Eight

There wasn't much time. All the ruckus we made surely alerted the deaders, so it was no surprise when we bolted out of the back door, arms loaded with bags, that in the distance was the jerky movements of an army of deaders headed for us.

My father opened the back doors of the van. It had once been white but was now caked in dirt and grime, maybe even some blood as dark rust-colored streaks ran up the sides. I feared the front bumper looked worse.

A stench from inside the van made me cringe. Blankets were piled in a corner, wrappers and empty bottles filled the empty space of the floor but pickers couldn't be choosers. We piled in. I lifted my shirt over my nose and attempted to breathe through my mouth. I'd gotten used to the zombie odor of death but not human B.O. It was almost worse. No, it *was* worse, because we were trapped inside a rolling metal cage with no side windows. It couldn't vent.

The small man appeared to be the only one not bothered by the odor as the rest of us had lifted our shirts over our mouths and noses. Obviously they'd been living inside it for a while.

My father hit the gas and the army of deaders receded further and further behind us. The port seemed a lot further away on foot then it was in a vehicle. Within minutes the van coasted to a stop.

The empty bottles rolled around, one hitting my foot and coming to a stop.

We loaded the dinghy and I untied the rope. My father stared at me. "Aren't you getting in?"

"Dad, we talked about this, and now we have wheels. We have somewhere to go. You get to the yacht and take care of Mom."

By the look in his eyes I knew he expected that from me but not Sarah who stood by my side. "I'm staying Mr. Smyth. They need my help."

"Sarah? This wasn't the agreement," his voice shook and his eyes bored into her then me.

She smiled. "It wasn't, but I can help. My mom is gone because of this thing, all this death has taken too many lives. I need to do my part, not hide on a yacht in luxury that masks how bad the world has become." She turned on her heel and walked back to the van.

"I love you, Dad. We have the radio. Don't worry." I blew him a kiss and joined Sarah at the van. The four of us piled inside, Heather at the wheel.

Once the doors were closed Heather looked over her shoulder at the small man. "There's a facility. A place they were testing zombies. What do you know?"

He scratched his head. "If that's so it was secret, not something announced on the news. How do I know where it is?"

The gun still on my person, I considered pulling it out, but wasn't much of a shot and that wouldn't be too great an idea in such a small space so I pulled my ax. "Think, or this will find a spot in your skull."

His eyebrows shot up. "OK, there's a place in the foothills. It's not easily accessible and surrounded by a gate but it could be what you're looking for."

Heather shot me a satisfied smile. "Lead the way."

Once she pulled onto the road he took us in a different direction than we took on foot for our grocery adventure. We went a couple blocks, turned, then another couple and turned. It felt as though he was leading us in circles.

Sarah, reading my mind, stated in her angry voice, "I don't think he bloody well knows anything. We aren't heading towards the foothills but weaving through the city. He's wasting time." She narrowed her eyes and glared at him in the front passenger seat. "My friend is pretty crazy. She'll slam that blade through your neck before you know what hit you. Don't play us."

He swallowed hard. "This is a longer route but the direct route is cluttered with cars and the dead. Everyone headed for the hills when it hit but the illness swept over the city in a matter of hours. They became walking dead before they could escape. One car wreck led to another and the people are still there, wandering."

"F--" I didn't get the word out before a loud pop exploded in my ear and the van veered to the left. In the back we slid to the right then were tossed forward as the van hit something hard and came to a stop.

"Is everyone alright?" Heather called as she maneuvered between the front seats into the back with us.

No one was hurt but the van wasn't going anywhere. The tire had blown and that caused Heather to lose control and smash into two cars stopped on the side of the road. As we surveyed the damage a horde of zombies was on the move towards us. "We gotta get out of here," I said, pointing at the stumbling beasts headed our way.

I handed the gun back to Heather and, with my ax in hand, pointed at the man. I wasn't giving him a chance to escape in case the enticement of the yacht wasn't enough. "We'll follow you."

He stuttered for a second, "Uh... I..." His eyes shifted from the deaders in the distance to me. "Sure."

Unless injured, one would have to purposely walk slower than a zombie to be caught by a group from behind. In no time the group of deaders were left in our dust. They weren't a threat but what awaited us ahead was.

We ducked through an alley. It was covered in body parts, chopped heads, and a couple wriggling bodies whose spinal cords hadn't quite been severed. They connected bodies to necks like wire. On the other side was a death zone. Vehicles strewn haphazardly across the roads. Shivers ran up and down my spine. The gory scene and obnoxious odor nearly knocked me to my knees.

A familiar drip drag shuffle caught my ears and I whipped around to see a zombie stumbling from the shadows teetering towards Sarah. She had a foot beside a severed leg and another foot beside a decapitated body. The zombie shuffled forward, tripping over its finally dead friends, somehow managing to stay upright.

Sarah was frozen in place. I jumped through the mess of body parts, hoping to reach her before the unsteady zombie. A shot rang out and the deader dropped. It's oozing head landing on Sarah's foot. I glanced at Heather who'd taken the initiative to fire her weapon. It served to kill the deader which might have been a good thing but it alerted others and the zombie drip drag echoed through my ears as more poured from the shadows following the sound.

The roads were coated with the things but this was worse. There wasn't a bare spot between them. "What have you led us into?" I snarled at the man.

"You think I would go first into a pile of zombies if I didn't think they weren't dead?" he growled back. The first time I'd heard him have backbone.

"You're an idiot, maybe so!" I argued. I didn't even know why. It clearly wasn't worth wasting my time, but rage boiled inside me as I thought of Sarah's near miss and the wall of zombies nearly surrounding us now.

"Quick, let's go!" shouted Heather as she bounced from one empty spot on the pavement to the next. Maybe we could slide through the openings between the vehicles but what awaited us on the other side? I grabbed Sarah's hand and pulled her along, attempting to follow Heather's path, only her legs were longer than ours.

I felt pressure on my ankle and something heavy as I lifted my right leg. Glancing down, a hand was grasped around my shin. It was attached to a partial torso. I shook it. Sarah grabbed it by the spinal cord and pulled. The spinal cord ripped from its body and went flying. It knocked a couple deaders off balance. Her wrinkled nose and gritted teeth displaying how grossed out she was.

We skipped through the bodies towards Heather who was on the other side of the sea of death. Zombies shuffled her way and she stood in a fighting stance, the gun poised in her hands ready to shoot some brains out.

I couldn't allow her to fight the throng of deaders alone and the sound would surely bring more. I also doubted she had enough bullets. Putting all grossness aside, I ran full force, my shoes squishing and sliding on jellied body parts. Heather cracked one on the skull, it dropped back, then another. I slid out my ax and joined her, dropping the blade beneath their skulls in order to sever their spinal cords. One by one they dropped, but more kept coming.

We were surrounded by them and clumsy and blind as they were we couldn't fight them all off, nor could I see to the other side of them. They formed a large mass with the four of us in the middle, fighting for our lives with crude but effective weapons.

The small man used a knife. He stuffed it into their skulls with precision but he didn't see the one behind that caught him on the shoulder. He spun around and shoved his blade through its neck but not before it took a chunk of his arm.

Fresh blood dripped from his wound. The deaders all but forgot about us as they surrounded him like a wall until he disappeared among them.

A blast ricocheted in my ears and chunks of metal and body parts rained down around us. An eyeball rolled down my shirt; even though it didn't touch my skin I felt its cool wetness. Through the mass of deaders, flames erupted and licked at a vehicle. Zombie heads turned in unison like we never existed and moved towards the explosion. They even forgot the fresh blood and feast they were having on the small man.

I felt my mouth drop open. Attracted to noise, the mindless beasts walked to their death. One, caught in the explosion but not completely destroyed, staggered into the flames, its right arm blown straight off. Another, missing most of its torso, intestines falling against its legs, fell into the flames.

One by one zombies dropped as bullets whizzed into their heads. Their brains painted the concrete. The only thing I knew could explain this turn of events was the military's presence. If that was the case they weren't collecting me today. My ears ringing from the explosion. I gasped as a huge black vehicle became visible and a vigilante group loaded with guns. They most definitely weren't military anyways as they were dressed in civilian clothing.

My mind a flurry, I didn't notice Heather until she put a hand on mine. I glanced into her eyes and watched her lips. I couldn't hear anything; my ears felt as though they hadn't popped after a long plane ride. Focusing on her lips, I couldn't make out what she was saying. Her hand moved from my arm to the group.

Straight ahead, the crowd of vigilantes parting, a man walked towards us. Not too tall but his form large and bulky, cowboy boots on his feet peeking from under his jeans. His white shirt as bright as the morning sun, unscathed by the devastation that surrounded us.

Chapter Nine

I stared ahead like a deer frozen in headlights. When the man in the white shirt got close enough I noted his straight nose and flared nostrils. His head held high, back straight as an iron rail, and unbreakable stride showed confidence. A grim expression creased his face.

In contrast to his blinding white shirt, a black strap crossed his shoulder carrying a weapon -- a rifle -- hung over his back. A belt around his chest carried a number of weapons. Heather ran towards him.

Like John Wayne saving the day in one of the westerns my dad was so fond of, he tipped the brim of his cowboy hat upwards and greeted Heather as she reached him.

I whipped my head around. Sarah stared at me blankly and took a large gulp. Simultaneously our eyes diverted to the small man. He lay gasping for breath, a chunk eaten from below his chest. Intestines falling out like uncooked sausage. I gasped.

The ringing in my ears continued. A hand touched my shoulder and an unfamiliar face, dark with wrinkles on the forehead and crow's feet around silky brown eyes. A man. I read his lips as they parted and moved. "He will turn."

Would he? It was a morbid thought and the small man was obviously in great pain but I wanted to know. *Did bites turn us into zombies?* I didn't think so. "Have you seen it happen?"

The man's brows lowered. "He's been bit."

"Does a bite turn people?" The man had more than a bite but would he die and come back or simply die.

"You want to wait and find out?" the man asked, loud enough I heard it through the ringing.

I nodded.

"We don't have time. More will come." He shot the small man in the head.

Great! Now I'd never know. I let out a breath. Sarah had joined Heather and they motioned for me to join them. We were smack in the middle of a new war zone; fresh deader bodies covered the road. The man grabbed my hand and we sifted through the wreckage until reaching the group that saved our hides.

Their mouths opened but I heard no words, instead I followed Heather's lead and we climbed into the back of the large black vehicle. Once everyone was piled inside the large cowboy man started the ignition and the vehicle moved. Bars covered the windows and bench seats without backs were all there was to sit on.

The ringing was so high pitched it sounded as if someone was screeching in my brain. Little by little it lessened to an annoying hum. I nervously picked at the bug repellant paint on my thumbnail, keeping an eye on the vigilantes. Highly allergic to mosquitoes, it wasn't the smartest move, so I tucked my hands beneath my butt.

Sounds started coming through but more as mumbles than actual speech so I used my sense of sight to take in the surroundings. We sailed past a sign with an airplane and continued towards a large building, passing shuffling zombies they shot on sight through the barred windows. It was no wonder dead deaders were everywhere, painting the landscape with death.

After what felt like an hour but was more like five or ten minutes the vehicle coasted into a parking garage and wound upwards until we reached the top deck.

The cowboy stepped around to the driver's side door and lowered his head inside. His top lip curled in a sort of smile. "You'll be safe here." The ringing so quiet now I heard his words through a tunnel.

I gave him a hard stare. "Are you military?" I saw no reason to waste time with formalities. They weren't taking me or at least not today.

He chuckled. "No. SAPS. At your service."

SAPS, what the heck was that South African Paramilitary Squad? My eyes twitched involuntarily. "What?"

"He's South African police," Heather followed up, her voice really loud. I assumed she was partially deaf too.

Before he could get a word out Sarah spoke, "What was that explosion? Geez, my ears are still ringing." Her voice a mix of irritation and gratefulness.

He shifted in his fancy boots. "A grenade. I loaded up." He patted his belt thick with weapons.

"I'm protecting the few who haven't turned. We have a small group but it's getting larger. I have a few tricks I keep with me. The ringing will go away shortly."

I gawked. *He and the others, without a doubt, were responsible for the road kill we ran into?* Not that it was a question. I'd already figured that out. Sarah and I stepped out of the vehicle and went through the formalities of introductions but it didn't last long, the cowboy man's name was Deavers. He guided us through the garage and towards an elevator. If they were the zombie death squad then we were in good hands.

"Where is everyone?" I asked. If there were more we needed to get everyone, and this guy, out. The SAPS might be able to help us get to the lab.

Sarah's wide eyes scanned the parking garage as we made our way around the bend.

Deavers didn't turn his head back as he talked. I figured he was like me, keeping an eye open for more deaders. "Not here. They're inside the airport. We've been holed up here for a couple weeks, cleared those things out and have plenty of food, space, a generator which provides us electricity. We even got a pilot."

Sarah walked in step with me. "So why haven't you left?"

"Where would we go? We have everything we need here." His boots didn't make a sound against the pavement. His step was silent as a ghost.

Heather walked in stride with Deavers. "The military has been taking everyone. The U.S. but maybe the world's combined forces..."

He cocked his head towards her, concern in his eyes, but he didn't break his stride and continued down the path. The garage was painted in brain matter and blood. The sun was beginning to shine through the dark clouds, pushing them away. At the end of the lot were two more SUVs, one tan and one red, with chain link fencing around the windows and bars across the grill and tail. Each had what looked like a bullhorn strapped to the top. It was like something seen in a movie.

Deavers folded his arms across his chest. "I'll take you where you need to go but not until you've had a good meal and your hearing returns to normal. This beast has capabilities to get through the thickest crowds of them but I need to know more before I send my men out." A heavy clue that he didn't naturally trust us even though he'd saved our lives.

Inside the airport they had limited power from generators. With a large supply of fuel stored for the airplanes they could go for a while before needing more. They kept the food cold and a kitchen working, along with hot water for showers and cleaning clothes which they hung to dry instead of eating up more power.

The gates were makeshift homes. It was an entire community with a dozen or so residents. Sarah and I were introduced to an older lady and left behind as Deavers and Heather, along with a couple other men, went to talk "adult". It wasn't like Sarah and I couldn't handle that I wasn't part of the plan but Heather gave me a look that said 'do as they ask'.

This wasn't our boat or our home. We were on their turf so I complied, my mind shouting a few nasty words and a roll of my eyes. The older lady, short and round, her graying hair tucked behind her ears, introduced herself as Dalila but to call her Lila.

My mind didn't hear much of what she said as it wondered if we should trust these people. Deavers saved our lives and Lila was obviously a gentle soul with her heartfelt smile and soft voice, but why had they separated us and when would we get to the reason we were in Cape Town?

Lila stopped when we got to a group of teens. It wasn't really a group but a couple. A boy and a girl, from the looks of them they were twins. Her sweet smile disappeared as her round lips introduced us, "Mazi, Mesi, this is Sarah and Maddie."

They stared at us with the same eyes, definitely twins. Lila teetered off, saying no more. Frustrated, I dropped into a seat across from them. Sarah followed my lead.

"So what's your story?" Mazi inquired. His face reminded me of a young Charles Michael Davis from the TV show *The Originals* and I had to admit he was smokin' hot. Sarah's mouth gaped. I nudged her in the side to bring her back to reality. She gave me a sideways glance.

"Searching for answers," I responded with a clipped voice.

Mesi's eyes shifted from Sarah to myself. "No need to be rude. Deavers found us and brought us here. He's a good guy. If it wasn't for him we'd be dead or like them."

Sarah shifted in her seat. "How soon did people start turning here?"

"After the swarm of black bugs took over the city," answered Mazi.

Sarah's face took on the dreamy look again. This time I let it go. She had the hots for him. So be it -- there wasn't much else out there to give anyone hope.

"The air was so thick with them and they stuck to everything, then the rains came and washed them all away," Mesi followed up with a far-off look in her eyes.

Mazi glanced at Sarah and they exchanged a look before Sarah realized she'd been made and shifted her eyes to the blank wall. "Us too," she said.

"So what do you do all day?" I asked.

Mesi shrugged. "This. Not much excitement in here and they won't let us out. They treat us like little kids." She rolled her eyes. "We have chores, everybody does them, but once we finish there's nothing and the adults won't let us in on anything. I feel like a prisoner but I'd rather be that than eaten by one of those things."

The way she said it, I doubted they really sat around and did nothing. Her distinct eye roll told me they knew more than the adults wanted them to. "You never spied on the adults?"

Mazi's lips curled at the ends. *Oh yeah, he was mischievous.* He glanced around us then leaned in, we followed his lead. "They go on these missions like the one when they found us, bringing in one person, two people, sometimes none but they kill those things by the dozens. Ramstein, Ramrod, and Bloody Mary --" I assumed was the other souped up SUV killing machine, "-- have blades that cut right through the middles of those things. They drop to the ground."

Sarah's eyes widened. "Have you ever left the airport?"

A sardonic smile crossed Mesi's lips. "We got this place and their routines figured out. At first we were happy to be alive and safe but we can't stay here forever. It's a false safety. There're more of them than us and I swear they're getting smarter. They like to hang out in the garage. The adults always leave the pilot here with Lila and us. I don't think they want to lose him like they have others."

The garage part wasn't news and these two obviously knew more than they let onto the adults. I guessed they trusted us since we were teens too. Maybe it was time to trust them. "What do you know about a top secret facility?"

Both furrowed their brows then Mazi spoke. "There's a place. It's on the outskirts, tucked into the foothills. I passed it before all this began. There's no name on the building, it doesn't have any windows and is surrounded by a metal fence."

"Can you get us there?" I asked. My mind a swarm of activity.

"Maybe," Mazi responded, "but we don't have weapons or a car and I don't want to walk it."

Sarah piped up and spewing confidence in me said, "Maddie's nickname is Zombie Girl and they didn't take our weapons."

My brain lit up, she was right. My ax, the shovel, the hoe were all in Ramstein along with tons of other weapons. All we needed were keys.

I filled everyone in on what Heather and I found on the thumb drive. Their eyes enlarged as they listened and we all agreed that we'd go on our own mission when they didn't expect it.

Chapter Ten

I clicked the radio off after a short conversation with my family. I filled them in on all the events and even over the staticky airwaves heard the fear and anxiety in my mother's voice. I dropped the radio to the table beside me.

Heather sat down in the airport seat next to me, her eyes searching my face. "We're going out first thing in the morning. You are not coming with us, Maddie."

I hid my sneer and went for the innocent, puppy dog approach. "Why not?"

Her hip jutted to the side and she folded her arms over her chest. "They won't allow it and I agree. Your parents are trusting me to keep both of you safe. You will stay here and not get any silly ideas to leave."

"Fine," I said in a defeated voice, clutching my hands in my lap. I had three willing people and weapons. All we needed was a mode of transport.

Heather narrowed her eyes and glanced from me to Sarah then to me. "That's it, no fight? I hardly believe that Maddie."

What was she, my parent? We'd broken into the thumb drive together as partners in crime and now I was feeling betrayed. I kept quiet.

Heather unfolded her arms. "Walk with me, Maddie."

I stood, sighed, and walked with her, keeping an arm's distance between us. At the moment I was more than displeased with her and she knew it.

"I told them all about the drive and its contents. If there's information there it will help us all. Like us, they are trying to survive. You are a curious, brave girl but you have to sit this one out." She walked in step with me then halted.

She turned and took my hands in hers. "They have the weapons and vehicle to offer the best protection. Much better than our makeshift ones. This area hasn't been cleansed. Zombies are out there. I need you and Sarah to be safe. Promise me you'll stay here."

Ughh... *Why were adults such experts at guilt tripping?* I'd come to think of Heather as more of a friend. That was probably my mistake and for the moment I thought against leaving.

Searching my face and reading it too well, she said, "Forget all that 'you're an adult now' stuff from your mom. You are still her little girl, Sarah too, and I have to keep you safe."

She was right. I glanced at the dried zombie blood on my clothing, bringing my mind back to the massive horde of zombies. They were everywhere in large numbers.

I thought of my family. The short radio conversation and I heard it in their voices. They wanted me safe, not slicing and dicing the dead and, as Heather suggested, they were counting on her. I blew out a breath. I couldn't let any of them down.

If my job was to stay here then, reluctantly, I would. "OK..."

Heather propped a hand on her hip. "That's not convincing, Maddie."

My mind had already switched gears as it made the decision to succumb to the adults' wishes. I now thought of the zombie illness and Eshe. *Sarah was bit too but never had any symptoms. Eshe's symptoms weren't like my father's but a nasty bacterial infection he was fighting from the wound itself.*

I considered Heather's words and they played through my head as I washed off in the makeshift shower. Swirls of red and pink raced down the drain until the water ran clear. I turned the faucet off and grabbed the clean towel, wrapping it around my body and patting myself dry. Clean clothes lay on the counter. They were a bit baggy but would do.

I laughed, full and loud, when I glanced at myself in the mirror. My hair hung thick, wet and tangled over my shoulders against the loose-fitting white shirt. Centered was a red symbol that looked like a medal an Olympian might have only it was red with a white star in the middle with the words *Etoile du Sahel.* I hadn't a clue what it meant. In my pre-zombie life I wouldn't have been caught dead in something like it but today I was happy to have something clean and devoid of blood and guts.

After dinner I gathered Sarah, Mazi, and Mesi together informing them about the change of plans. Sarah's mouth dropped in surprise.

"That's it? We're not going on a mission?" Sarah inquired, a brow lifted in curiosity and disbelief.

I twisted my mouth as I faced incredulous yet relieved stares from the group. "We should stay here. We'll be more help instead of causing more harm. They'd search for us if we left." I sighed.

Mazi shoved his hands into the front pockets of his jeans and leaned against the wall behind him. "You're chickening out." Mischief twinkled in his eyes.

Sarah twirled to face him. "Maddie is not!" she said, standing up for me.

"So we're going to stay here like always as the adults do their *thing*." He pushed off the wall and stalked away.

He was right. *Who snuck off and discovered the military's involvement and a yacht to carry them out of Morocco? Who had the premonition and stocked up her father's boat for a trip away from zombie-infested Jacksonville?* And now I was making the decision to be complacent, allowing the adults to guilt trip me. "We need a vehicle."

Mazi's lips turned up in a smile. He dug a hand into a front pocket of his jeans and tugged, pulling a short silver chain out of his pocket with a shiny key. "We got a ride."

Chapter Eleven

That night, I tossed and turned, an ache in my gut. Masses of zombies swarmed after Heather, chasing her down. Their legs moving swiftly beneath them. I shot upwards, sweat dripping from my forehead. I let out a deep breath as it was only a dream. A horrible nightmare. Sarah lay on the makeshift bed next to mine, snoring quietly.

Dropping my head onto the pillow, I took several deep breaths, returning my heart rate to normal. My vivid dreams started with the premonition I shared with Bryce. Sarah and my parents were zombies. Bryce and I were the only living souls. We saved their lives when the real apocalypse started because of that dream. The cold metal of the compass I brought out of the dream was a constant reminder of it and Bryce.

Bryce, *what was he doing right now? Had they reached Norfolk? Could I force my mind to reach out to him so we could connect again in a dream?* So many questions. I clutched the compass and envisioned Bryce in my mind. His green eyes smiling and wind blowing loose strands of his chestnut hair that escaped the ponytail.

My body eased and I dropped into slumber, willing my mind to reach him but as dreams go my mind had thoughts of its own. The ocean below soared like a bird following the white cap of the wake from a sleek silver yacht. The water teamed with fish. A sudden blast of several birds dive-bombed the waters in search of food, grabbing the fish. I was part of the flock and, against my will, followed their lead, veering straight into the waters.

Beneath the surface I suddenly became human and sunk, salt stinging my eyes. "Bryce," I called, moving my arms to propel myself to the surface of the water. When I broke through the sun was on me and I was on the deck of the yacht. Voices from inside the bridge grabbed my attention and I turned my head backwards glancing into the room.

Bryce! I jumped to my feet and ran to the bridge, finding it empty. *Where was he?* I searched each room. The voices one step ahead of me until I went full circle back to the bridge. There he stood at the wheel. His long hair pulled back, blowing from the ocean breeze. I walked forward, tapping him on the back. He turned, his face lighting up. He wrapped his arms around me and held tight. It felt real; he felt real. His heart beating against me, his folded arms drawing me closer.

I didn't want to let go and lose the moment but I wasn't here to lose my bearings in his embrace. Pushing out of it but keeping him in arm's reach I searched his eyes. "Where are we?"

"How are you here?" he asked, ignoring my question.

"It's a dream. I thought about you and I'm here." It felt as strange saying it as it was in reality. *Was this really happening, or only in my mind?*

Something tickled my shoulder and when I reached my hand across it I felt another hand. Turning abruptly I stared to face the half-eaten fleshy mess of a zombie. I didn't have a weapon so I jumped towards Bryce but he was gone. The scent of his soap lingering in the air.

"Maddie," called his voice from somewhere far off and through what sounded to be a tube. The hand reached over my shoulder again. The zombie was suddenly behind me. I squeezed my fist around the handle of my ax but it wasn't my ax instead a chunky black phone.

"Maddie!"

I recoiled and my eyes fluttered open. Sarah eyed me curiously. "You were dreaming."

I took a minute to gain my bearings. *Was that really Bryce?* His arms around me felt so real, and the fresh scent of the soap he used, but it was a dream. The premonition was something different and felt completely real. Sarah dropped onto the bed beside me. Mazi and Mesi stared at me with curious eyes.

"What's happening?" I asked, suddenly frantic that something was wrong.

"Time to go. In the early hours there're only two guards and no one is watching the trucks. They're looking for zombies," Mesi offered.

They'd done their research. We slept in our clothes and, following Mazi, slipped through the airport. We crossed the gates and went through a door that led to areas of an airport I'd never seen. The halls were filled with offices and closed doors.

We scooted up a set of stairs and Mazi turned when we reached the top, making a hand gesture to stop. We bunched against the wall. Mazi gestured to a door across the corridor, pointed towards the end of it and mouthed 'guard'.

I poked my head around the corner. The guard wasn't looking in our direction but would surely hear us crossing the hallway as he wasn't more than ten feet away. He was a big guy, at least six feet tall and easily two hundred and fifty pounds with his bulky muscles. I glanced again at the door on the other side of the corridor. It was so close; if I leaned out I could nearly touch it. We needed a distraction.

The squawk of a radio caught me off guard and I jumped. A voice came through. "Taking a coffee break, cover my post."

"10-4," responded the bulky guard. He turned and I pulled my head back.

Behind us was a door. Mesi already had it open. We scooted inside and gently closed the door. Hefty footfalls echoed on the tile floor and a door creaked open. It was too close to be any other door than the one we needed.

Mazi poked his head out the door and, without turning, he slipped out. I followed behind and watched as he propped a knife against the door frame. He turned and his eyes grew wide as he didn't expect to see me.

I turned to see Sarah and Mesi behind me, staring expectantly. One by one we scooted through the door to the garage. Keeping to the shadows, we moved toward the trucks.

The guard nowhere in sight as if he'd vanished or, most likely, taken the elevator. The trucks were a mere thirty feet or so from us. To my right was the edge of the garage and to the left the exit. I wasn't without ideas or the sinking feeling deaders could be lurking in the dark corners of the garage.

Scanning the area, a tire iron was leaned against the wall. I picked it up. Mazi, Mesi, and Sarah stared ahead towards the vehicles as if willing to take the risk, only it would surely send the adults after us in a hurry instead of allowing them to wake normally and find us not there. We'd be robbed of time and I wasn't going to let that happen.

Easing my way to the edge of the garage, I peered down and flung the tire iron over the edge. It didn't sail far into the air and dropped hard. I waited a minute, no radios. Footsteps to my left told me the group was heading towards the truck. I continued watching below and when I saw the shadow of someone round the corner of the garage I ran toward the truck. Mazi had already started the motor and Sarah held the door open for me. I jumped in and pulled the door closed as Mazi shifted into gear.

With the lights off, we coasted downward and onto the road. Mazi didn't turn the lights on until we were a good distance from the airport. I kept my eyes peeled out the back window and when no one followed I finally let out a sigh of relief.

It wasn't Ramstein, but the truck was loaded with weapons, mostly guns, but beneath the seats were also rounds of ammo and katanas. I pulled one out of its sheath. The hilt comfortable in my hand as if made for it. The blade shone in the moonlight. I grabbed the strap and tossed it over my back.

Sarah and Mesi also garnered katanas. For a female, they were a good weapon; lightweight, sharp, and extremely effective for slicing through skin and muscle.

"Have you ever killed a zombie?" I asked, jumping into the front seat. I figured I had the most experience here.

"No," Mazi said reluctantly. "We mostly stayed hidden until Deavers found us and we've been locked up in the airport since."

That's about what I figured. No surprise there. "They're slow and walk with jerky movements. They can't see but they're attracted to noise and some smells, especially blood. The most effective way of killing them is to get them at the base of the spinal cord. It'll stop all the automatic functions in their bodies. The ones that sustain them. With a severed spinal cord, there's no heartbeat, breathing stops, and they drop to the ground like a sack of rotting trash."

Mesi's eyes widened and she scrunched her face. Maybe this wasn't the best idea. We were in a zombie death machine on our way to a lab, without any knowledge of what we'd find there, with people who had limited to no zombie killing experience.

Zombies loitered in the roads in small groups as we flew past them. Their bodies mottled in bites with missing chunks of flesh and torn clothing. The truck lights beamed on a thin blonde woman shuffling down the middle of the road. In one hand she held a red can. As we neared, I noted it was a diet pop. I chuckled as that was possibly the strangest zombie thing I'd seen yet and wondered if she was even aware of the can in her hand.

Mazi shifted the tires to go around her.

"Put her out of her misery. Hit her straight on," I suggested.

He narrowed his eyes. "You want me to hit her?"

"Yeah. Look at her. Would you want to live that way?"

He hit the gas and plowed into her. She hit the grill with a crunch and bounced over the windshield and top of the SUV, landing with a thunk on the pavement behind us. I wasn't sure that had killed her, remembering the ones I'd run over in my dream, but possibly it gave her enough head trauma she'd die quickly. It didn't sound compassionate, but was. Their quality of life stunk, figuratively and literally.

Mesi gasped when the zombie flew over the SUV and pulled a hand to her mouth. The diet pop can flew into the air and landed somewhere unseen.

Bloody Mary, designed for slaying zombies, cruised over the zombie-splattered roads headed to the facility. Soon enough we were out of the city and heading into the mountains, following a deserted road. No zombies shuffled the roads, no animals lurked in the trees, and no cars loitered. It was void and empty.

We rolled to a stop outside a large, nondescript, gray building surrounded by a twelve foot or so security fence. Zombies loitered and wandered the parking lot beyond the fence, trapped like bugs in a box. When they heard Bloody Mary they sprinted in a fast-paced drip-drag to the fence. It zapped them and they jittered then dropped, convulsing on the ground. Most of them were in lab coats and business-wear.

Chapter Twelve

A young woman, a three inch heel on one foot and nothing on the other, hobbled towards the fence, tripped on the spasming pile and dropped to the ground. Many more stagger-ran in the same direction. Then changed their pattern. I stared in disbelief as they stopped walking into the fence and tripping over the spasming ones. Instead they halted short of the ones on the ground and circled the fence.

Was this on purpose? Were they somehow messaging each other or learning? The thoughts horrified me but also made me more curious.

"There's electricity in the building," suggested Mazi with a smirk on his face as he eyed the convulsing zombies.

Mesi furrowed her brow. "Probably a generator, but we need to get through so we'll have to cut the power."

"No, no! We can't do that. We might need it and without it anything can get inside the building," Sarah said, her voice frantic, edging on horrified.

Mesi let out a deep breath. "How else do you suggest we get in?"

Sarah pursed her lips in annoyance. "This truck is full of weapons. There has to be something?"

We searched every nook and cranny of Bloody Mary. The glove box, center console, overhead compartments, and beneath the seats. I found a chunky phone, it reminded me of the old fashioned ones everyone lovingly called bricks, and a radio. I figured I'd keep it. My father being the cell phone expert I figured he'd know if we could use it and the radio I clipped around my waist since Heather had the other.

It was Sarah that found the floor compartment. She slid it open and inside was what we needed. Grenades. *I'd never used one but how hard was it to pull a pin and toss it?*

There was also a tool bag. I opened it up and my eyes immediately went to the bolt cutters. "I don't think we need to blast the fence," I said, pulling the bolt cutters out of the bag.

Mazi shot a glance at me while parking his arms over his chest. Sometimes actions spoke louder than words.

"The cutting part is metal but the handle is rubber. It won't conduct electricity," I pointed out.

The left side of Mazi's mouth lifted in a curl. "We need to create a diversion. Mesi is going to toss a grenade over the fence into the middle of the yard. They'll instinctively move towards it and Sarah you will knock the lock off the gate. Maddie and I will go in together -- weapon to weapon."

Exactly what I was thinking, except I saw myself tossing the grenade. She counted one, two, three and thrust it. It crashed into the yard with a bang. Sarah gripped the bolt cutters and snapped them against the lock on the gate, it sparked and a voice mixed with static squawked. The voice broke up before I could make out the words, judging by everyone else's actions, neither could they. Grasping the bolt cutters again, Sarah squeezed with all the might in her muscles the lock broke free. She pushed it open. Mazi and I entered back to back.

Zombies milled around the explosion, a few missing body parts that had been attached before.

Mazi winced at the sight and caught a double-headed ax into the neck of a deader who dropped forward, pulling another off balance. I was a bit jealous of his cool weapon of choice, then thought about how heavy it must be and decided the katana was a much better option. He spun and hit another while yet another fell towards him. Mazi stuffed one side of the ax into the carotid artery of a zombie, blood spraying everywhere, while the other fell into my sword and dropped as I sliced through its spinal cord.

The zombie with the missing three inch heel limped towards us. I kicked her in the gut. She lost her balance and fell to the ground. I swung across her neck. It sliced so effortlessly and didn't stick in the flesh. I was really getting used to this lightweight, longer-range weapon.

Within minutes we'd cleared the lot. "Good work," I said, dropping the katana to my side. For a newbie he wasn't bad and had a flair for slicing the dead.

He let out a long breath, his eyes scanning the collection of deaders as if surprised at his own accomplishment.

The voice at the gate continued but the static made the message unclear. It sounded like gibberish.

Sarah and Mesi joined us. "What now? How do we get inside?"

My eyes scanned the bloody mess of zombies strewn across the yard. Mazi strode to the building and tilted his head as he eyed the lock. "Good question. We could beat it open with the bolt cutters."

Leave that comment to a man. *Brawn and no brains.* "No, it has a key pad." An idea was bubbling to the surface of my brain. A strong breeze blew a chunk of hair into my face. I pushed it out of the way. "Check those in lab coats. One of them probably has a key."

Sarah leaned down and slipped her hand into the pocket of one such lab coat attached to a tall man. His blank eyes stared straight into the early morning sky. The sun broke through the clouds and was baking the piles of deaders who were smelling more rancid by the second. With a grimace she dug her hands through all his pockets.

We all joined her and moved from one onto another. I glanced down at a large deader. His name tag connected to his pocket protector said "Pumper". Light brown-gray hair flopped over the side of his head in a fashion making it appear as if someone had left his head half-scalped. His fingers stuck in an awkward circle between his thumb and forefinger. I felt into his pocket and noted two thin plastic cards stuffed into it.

I pulled them out and glanced at the plastic cards, both appeared to be key cards like the one Eshe had kept from the scientist that I hadn't thought to steal from Heather. "Found something!" I shouted, straightening my back into a full standing position and flashed them over my head.

Sarah, Mazi, and Mesi halted their search and followed me to the door. I swiped a card through the credit card type swiper. Nothing happened. I tried the next card. This time it flashed a message *'Thumbprint needed to proceed'.* My eyes shot back to the deader I got the cards from. He was a large guy. *Darn!* "I need his hand."

I was met with grimaces, then Sarah nodded her head and marched toward "Pumper". She laid the sword across his wrist and made a couple practice slices then bore down. Sarah cringed as it dropped and, with a crunch of bones snapping, cut it clean off at the wrist.

She grabbed the hand and marched to the door, a grimace painted on her face. She didn't look at it once. Stuffing his thumb against the pad, the lock clicked. I was shocked to say the least. Sarah didn't even cringe when she pushed the finger against the key pad. I motioned for everyone to get behind me. Before I pushed the door open I glanced at the hand. "We may need to keep it."

That's when dismay showed on Sarah's face. "Really, Maddie?"

"Yes," I confirmed.

The building had no windows and the darkness was lit only by minimal security lighting. I carried the katana like I'd seen in the movies.

The fuzzy voice squawked again. The message boomed from all around but was still impossible to decipher. Chills ran down my back as we stalked into the dimly lit building. The door pushed closed behind us, sending another wave of chills prickling my spine. The room was small. To the right was a desk, a flat screen monitor set atop it. To the left was a blank wall and ahead was a long corridor.

Their first order of business was making sure the place was empty of deaders and, oddly enough, it lacked their rancid odor. Staying close, we entered the corridor. A number of doors were to the left and right, no windows inside the rooms.

Mazi shone his light towards a door. It had the same key card entry as the entrance. He kicked it but it didn't budge. Continuing down the hallway he tried all the doors the same way.

I wondered about the voice. *Where was it coming from? Was somebody alive alive in the place?*

We neared the end of the corridor. I turned, one wall was vacant of anything. I assumed it was an outside wall. The other had more doors and ahead at the end was a large glassed-in room. It also had emergency lighting and it flashed like something in a nightclub.

Mazi pulled something from his waistband; flashes of light caught a glint of the metal barrel of a gun in his hand.

"Do you even know how to fire that thing?" Sarah asked, a hand on her jutted hip. I thought the same thing.

He rolled his eyes. "Yes. My father taught me. Stay here."

When he reached the glass room he shined the light into it and scanned then pointed at me and Sarah for the key card and hand.

I swiped the key card and Sarah reluctantly lifted the zombie hand she been carrying by the loose fleshy part and pressed its finger against the pad once more. The glass door opened. The staticky voice blasted overhead and the stench of death eased into my nostrils. Mazi entered, leg over leg and gun scanning the room, he eased forward. Something was in there.

I followed behind him. He was showing how brave he was but I didn't think he was that smooth or efficient with a gun. When a shot rang then ricocheted across the room I knew my gut was right. I ducked below a metal table. "Are you trying to kill us?"

I lifted my head above the table and between light blinks spotted Mazi face to face with someone else. Not really a someone anymore, judging by its nose-clenching odor. I tapped my sword against the metal table and it pinged. The zombie turned clumsily and stumbled my way.

Mazi stared at me, gun poised in both hands at the back of the deader. I noted his hands quiver as he lowered the gun. When the deader got close enough, I spotted its clean lab coat and name tag. Jennings. It was female. Its hair fell from a bun on top of its head and it wore nurse shoes on its feet. I swung the sword. It went clean through. Her head dropped one direction and her body the other.

"I didn't know those blades were that sharp," Mazi said as he joined me.

"Me either." I shrugged.

Computers and various expensive lab equipment, test tubes, and other tools of science and doctors was stationed on the slick, stainless steel table and counter tops. The walls sterile white. This was it. If there were answers in this building they'd be in here.

I didn't know exactly what we were searching for but figured between the four of us we'd find something.

Chapter Thirteen

Heather paced nervously, imagining all types of danger and zombies munching on Maddie and Sarah. She'd asked her not to go and thought sincerely she wouldn't; and to take Mazi and Mesi too... She reminded herself over and over that Maddie would be fine. She knew zombies and how to kill them but thoughts of hordes surrounding them on all sides crept into her mind.

Heather pushed the button on the radio and before she got the words 'Maddie come in' out of her mouth a male voice filled with angst hollered.

"Quick now, everyone!"

Catching herself with a hand against the back of a chair Heather spun around. Footfalls from the men echoed through the gates. She followed.

"Now, now, now!" A man -- she thought his name was Logan -- shouted as they passed Lila, and a couple other ladies, waving his free hand in a motion for them to follow. *What was so urgent?*

The pilot stood in the doorway leading to one level of the garage. "I heard noise, shuffling, banging. When I checked I spotted two people tied up in the garage, hanging from the ceiling like sitting ducks," the pilot shot out in one breath.

They all picked up our pace and sprinted into the garage.

"Who would do that?" Heather asked.

"No one," Deavers answered as he opened the door leading to the garage. They halted their pace and stared at the couple tied up, hanging from the ceiling. "We can't go out there unarmed. It's got to be a trap and those people are bait."

Eyes shifted from one person to the next then Heather took it upon herself. "I'm going back for an ax or weapon. I suggest we all find something sharp or thick and blunt."

Deavers spoke up, "I'm always armed." He pulled a blade from his pocket and a gun from a holster.

Another man joined him, a blade in his hand too. Together they entered the garage. Heather followed behind. *These people might need medical attention*, she told herself, but truly was just curious. If they needed medical attention she'd give them that inside.

One, a woman who looked about thirty, her enlarged brown eyes embedded in a heavily freckled face followed the group's movements. Her blouse shredded at the shoulders and skirt covered in blood. The other was an older man, his face as freckled as hers, his hair gray and clothes tattered. They'd obviously been trying to survive the apocalypse until a deranged individual captured them.

Why? That was Heather's question. *Why on Earth, with times so desperate, would someone use these people as bait?*

Knowing better than to speak, the men gestured to each other. Their goal was to get these people untied as quickly as possible and inside the safety of the airport. Heather walked in stride with Deavers'. "Cover my back. I'll untie them."

He nodded and gave her his blade.

Her ears prickled in alert when she heard scuffling from a dark corner. She gulped, shot Deavers and the other man a glance and stepped towards the noise, leaving the people hanging from the rafters. As she grew closer her eyes adjusted to the dark corner and she made out the form of a human. It scuttled into the corner away from her.

It's human not deader. A zombie wouldn't run from me. The shadowy form could be the monster responsible for tying those people to the rafters. It scooted into the corner, its hands wrapped around its knees and eyes peering at her from between its knee caps. *It was a child!*

Stay cool, Heather, she reminded herself to quell the overwhelming urge to save the child. It could be turning or it could have a weapon but it appeared scared. "I'm going to help you," she whispered, putting her hand out, palm up in a peaceful gesture.

Its wide eyes widened further and stared beyond her. Heather knew that look. Spinning around she spotted the *drip drag* shuffle from the other side of the garage. *Crap!*

Deavers and the other man had spotted them too and were already lowering the woman from the rafters. The old man was already down. The group ran towards the door and Deavers towards Heather. From his pocket he grabbed a grenade and tossed it as the zombies shuffled from out of the shadows.

Flames licked the air and the loud kaboom made everyone's ears ring, temporarily deafening them. Deavers wrapped his hand around Heather's as she leaned towards the child in the corner, taking a chance, and grabbed one of its hands wrapped tightly around its knee and pulled. Like a train they pushed toward the door leading back to the safety of the airport.

The child scampered alongside Heather, two steps for every one of hers. Deavers took notice, letting go of her hand and grabbing the child from under its armpits. Zombies, partially burned, body parts blown off, emerged. From the doorway the pilot took pot shots aimed for their heads. Heather's mind focused on the door, she didn't look back to see how many he downed. She stayed focused, rushing through the door on Deavers' heels.

Making a quick head count, Heather slammed the door shut and dropped the makeshift bar across it as the sound of zombies slamming into it echoed in her ears between the ringing from the explosion.

"It won't hold," shouted the pilot as he rushed away, returning with a loaded luggage cart. Each of them grabbed whatever was close and piled it against the door. The slamming stopped and they moved away, unsure how many were out there or if they were moving on. The group rushed towards the gates followed by everyone else in the airport.

The lady they found in the garage spoke nervously in a language other than English, her words quick as Lila tried to calm her.

"She says 'thank you'. They were sure they were dead," Lila spoke towards the group as they caught their breath.

"Ask her... who did it." said the pilot between breaths. Obviously physical exercise wasn't necessary to fly a plane.

The lady spoke again. Her words calmer at first, then quicker.

"She says someone jumped them. They didn't see his face and they woke up tied to the rafters in the garage," Lila interpreted.

It turned out the lady and older man were father and daughter. The child was her son. The little boy didn't speak. He sat quietly, crouched on the floor.

Heather swallowed then grabbed the radio.

Maddie

I ordered everyone to load the test tubes and samples into a tub and took to checking the rooms. In the dimly lit hallway I opened the first door, clamping my hands around the katana's hilt. It was set up like an operating room, on the table was a dead deader. It's body turned to jelly and dripping onto the floor into puddles.

I cringed my face in disgust and stepped into the hallway. The next room contained another deader, this one emaciated but still living, sort of, and strapped to the table. Its neck, as well as its appendages, was held onto the table with chains.

Its fingers wiggled as I neared, as if attempting to grab me. A steel doctor's cart was near the bed and a hefty gas saw lay on top. I picked it up and dropped it over the face of the deader. Its face caved in and the saw clunked to the ground. I stepped out of the way to avoid losing my toes. It would have been smarter to filet its neck with the katana. I shrugged. It was now truly dead.

Room after room, I found one deader after another, some alive-ish, others clearly dead and missing various important organs such as their brains, hearts, and spinal columns. No sign of what the scientists did with the organs.

I returned to the glass room where everyone else waited. Vials, journals, needles, and equipment stacked neatly into a plastic tub. I glanced at them, a glass jar in my hand. Inside was a black heart.

Sarah opened her mouth to speak when groaning from outside the building stopped her short. We turned on our heels and rushed down the corridor.

Chapter Fourteen

Heather hadn't forgotten about Maddie. In that moment she grabbed a radio.

"Maddie, come in." She didn't hide the anger in her voice.

The radio buzzed in response and Maddie's voice came through, "Before you say anything, I'm sorry. We collected everything-" Maddie's voice was soon drowned by crashes and booms.

"To the planes. We have to go," Deavers ordered.

"Not without the kids." Heather stood her ground then depressed the button on the radio, "Maddie, are you there?"

An explosion crackled through the radio. "I'm here," Maddie responded.

Heather worried for her sake. It sounded like they'd met their own set of problems but she wasn't leaving without them. "You need to hurry back. The deaders are here. A group brought them. They've surrounded us. Be careful!" Heather crooned into the radio as the group headed through the gates and towards a plane.

The radio buzzed. "Maddie! Maddie!" Heather yelled with no response.

Thumping over their heads made her mouth drop and like a wave all their eyes moved towards the ceiling. "To the last gate. Go! Go!" ordered Deavers.

The pilot wrung his hands in anxiety. "You can fly a passenger plane, right?" asked Heather.

He cringed. "My license doesn't cover large passenger planes and we have no one to man the tower or navigate us. It's better we take my plane," he said as if he'd thoroughly considered this option in the past.

Deavers grabbed the pilot by the collar. "You said you could fly one of these. That bag of junk you call a plane won't get us off this continent."

The pilot's eyes wide, his chest heaved in short, labored breaths. "I lied. I thought it made me useful enough to keep me but my plane will get us wherever we need to go."

Deavers set him down and through clenched teeth said, "We need to get to the U.S. If that chunk of metal gets us off the continent. How long before we have to stop for gas?"

The pilot swallowed, sweat beading on his forehead. "I... I... It'll get us there."

Deavers harrumphed and the pilot shuddered.

Heather stepped in. "We don't have time for this. I hear them. We need to get out of here now."

Masses of zombies pushed against the airport and shuffled through the halls. They were on the roof but the runway was empty. They made a quick dash, grabbing food and weapons. The pilot opened the outside door to the gate closest to his plane and followed the ramp. One by one, everyone followed until they were in the belly of a passenger jet.

Why couldn't we take this plane? Was flying it really that different? It was large with plenty of seating and could accommodate all of them in comfort but today's zombie world was about surviving, not luxury, and she wasn't going with them.

She'd wait for Maddie and Sarah. They'd take the vehicle the kids stole and head towards the docks back to the boat. There was electricity on the boat and a computer. She had what she needed to study whatever they brought back. In the thick of the action, the thought of scolding Maddie hadn't eluded her but it would wait.

The pilot placed his hands over his eyes as he peered outside the plane. "We can slide down the emergency exit. There's an empty baggage truck. We can load up on it and take it to my plane."

Those trucks didn't move too fast but so long as they were faster than the zombies… They had many advantages to the deaders. First they could see; they were also faster and more agile. She'd follow their plan and help everyone onto the plane.

The pilot released the emergency hatch. A blow-up slide puffed out in front of them, hissing like an angry cat. The pilot went first. When he reached the ground he studied the area, searching the roof then the grounds for any deaders. Noting it clear, he waved them forward then directed everyone to an empty luggage truck.

Heather held her arms in an x over her head, an ax like Maddie's in one hand as she took the plunge and slid to the bottom of the slide. Getting off was the trick. The edge was puffy. She flopped her legs over the side and the pilot grabbed for her hands. She made it over the edge, teetering on one foot.

The pilot grabbed the ax from her hand then dropped it as a reaction to her wobble and the clink on the cement alerted the hoard of deaders on the roof. *Oh crap!*

Her breath caught as several zombies dropped from the roof, their skulls cracking against the cement. Blood poured in a trail and she sighed relief when she knew they wouldn't be getting back up; at least not those ones.

Deavers was the last to slide. He plummeted as she grabbed the ax. The second batch of zombies dropped, landing safely on top of the kamikaze deaders who took the plunge first. Rolling off the lifeless deaders, they staggered towards them.

The pilot waved for Heather and Deavers to get on the luggage truck. Deavers clutched Heather's hand and dragged her towards it as a growing number of staggering deaders moved their way. The low rumble of the engine caught their attention and they drifted towards them.

"We have to run for it," Heather suggested. "If we take the truck they'll surely follow because of the low rumble of the engine."

The pilot wrinkled his brows. "What?"

"They follow noise," Heather repeated, wondering how he'd survived without knowing that. The truck lurched forward and they followed. "I'll drive it while everyone else runs for safety," Heather suggested.

Deavers lowered his brows. "You're getting on the plane."

Of course! "Well, yeah. I can run faster than them," she lied. He knew she wasn't getting on. It didn't matter -- she'd get back to the boat.

Heather maneuvered the cart in the opposite direction of the plane. The sight of it made her cringe. It was a green tin can. "Maddie, come in Maddie," Heather shouted into the radio.

"Almost there," Maddie's voice sounded through static.

"Everyone else is getting on the plane," Heather responded. Deaders stagger-ran behind the cart. It didn't move fast but was quicker than them. She continued as the small plane fired up. Heather didn't look back but continued her steadfast five mile an hour journey across the runways.

A low rumble echoed against her ears as a red SUV -- Bloody Mary, blades all around whirling -- smashed through the fence and headed towards her, along with a mess of deaders.

Bloody Mary plowed through the mass of deaders following Heather. Their torsos disconnected from their legs, long cords of intestines and rivers of blood trailed after them as they used their arms to propel themselves forward, grasping at the cement. Inch by inch they continued to move.

The unsliced ones continued their stagger-run as they chased after Bloody Mary. Sprays of bullets streamed behind from the back window, dropping most of the deaders still on their feet. As the lethal SUV reached Heather it spun to a stop. The door opened and she jumped off the cart. Rolling to the ground, she scrambled to her feet and into the back of the SUV.

Deavers stood at the plane's door and Heather waved and shouted, "Jacksonville, Florida!" Then slammed the door shut.

He nodded his head and shouted it back only, with all the noise, Heather wasn't sure he got it right. The ladder of the plane closed and it coasted over the runway and into the sky. Heather wondered if she'd meet them again.

Chapter Fifteen

Bryce and Jack somewhere between Morocco and Norfolk

They'd been over the water two weeks, hadn't suffered any bad weather and maintained a reasonable amount of gas. Jack bartered the "reasonable" amount in his mind. They'd most likely make it on what they had but lost sight of the USS America. He was also reasonably sure it was heading to Norfolk as planned.

They'd successfully trapped the rat as it went for the wriggling fish bait as planned. Bryce dropped the lid, ensnaring the little beast. That was the easy part. They carried it onto the deck and the plan was to toss it over the side but they reconsidered. It wasn't like it could swim and zombie humans dropped like rocks in water but fresh bait might bring the zombie shark swimming their direction. The idea of a shark that was either living or nonliving sent chills up Jack's spine every time he thought about it.

Jack ended up lifting the lid while Bryce brought down a hammer they'd found in the engine room as they searched to be sure there wasn't any more zombie stowaways of any species. The force Bryce used to drop the head of the hammer crushed its tiny skull that was buried inside the hole it ate in its bait. Tuna guts mingled with rat brains spread across the water in the bucket.

Jack swallowed his vomit and glanced away from the disgusting sight as they lifted the bucket and dropped the contents over the side. It wasn't until later that either of them considered the speed at which the zombie rat moved. The human zombies they'd run across moved with quirky mechanical movements, but not the rat or what they'd seen of the shark. Like everything else, it didn't make a lick of sense. And neither could explain why other animals they'd seen weren't zombies. It could be the non-zombie animals were pickier about what they ate.

Bryce and Jack took turns at the helm. When one slept the other was awake as they sailed through the night. Jack, the more experienced sailor, took the night shift as it was trickier steering with only the light from the stars and moon to guide them. The golden sun lingered on the horizon causing Jack to squint his eyes. Silver twinkles blinked at him from the top of the water.

The sleek design of the yacht reminded Jack of a bullet so that's what he named it, ignoring the actual name painted in copper lettering on the side. His mind not so far away he didn't hear Bryce walk onto the bridge. The young man sunk into the chair beside him and Jack pulled his arms out from behind his head and shifted into a straight position grabbing the plate of food he'd brought.

It was their routine. When their shift was beginning that person made a meal; enough for two. They ate together and talked, reviewing their shift.

The rat incident was the most excitement they'd seen so far but neither was dismayed by that.

Bryce chewed then swallowed a bit of his spam sandwich. He'd learned -- they'd all learned -- real quick that food was a commodity and to eat whatever they could get their hands on that wasn't alive during or since the outbreak or needed refrigeration. That left canned and boxed goods. It was important to keep their energy levels up. "How far ahead of us do you think that ship is?"

"I reckon it's already in the port," Jack said matter-of-factly. "We got about another week if this weather keeps up." He lifted the sandwich to his lips and crunched down on a large bite.

Bryce grabbed a pair of sunglasses off the console and placed them over his eyes. Whoever's yacht it was before they stole it kept pairs in every room and now most were collected on the bridge. "How about gas?"

Jack's lip lifted causing his left eye to scrunch. He wiggled his fingers. "I think we can make it. There's not much between here and there so I don't think we have much choice."

They'd been cruising at speeds in excess of twenty knots and would have chosen to move faster, especially since experiencing great weather, but didn't want to waste gas. It was a valuable resource to them and wouldn't be so easy to fill in the middle of the Atlantic. There was also the likelihood the carrier knew they were following. The yacht was quicker and easier to turn around than a large carrier, even a smaller one like the USS America.

Once they approached Norfolk it would be a
different story but they didn't plan on waltzing into
the military' backyard, maybe even docking further
south and stealing a vehicle. Neither really knew
what to expect when they got there or even what
they'd do. There was no way to plan for it.

Jack lifted from his seat and stretched, patting
Bryce on the back as he relinquished control. Being
men, neither said anything, just grunting and glances
to acknowledge the switch in shift. Bryce didn't
know how Jack spent his time alone on the bridge
but Bryce spent his doing push-ups and running in
place. He needed to build his stamina and strength
sailing into the unknown.

At this point he wasn't making assumptions that
the U.S. was cleared like they'd witnessed in
Morocco. The U.S. was a large country with vast
expanses of land, meaning it might be impossible to
clear all the zombies, maybe the large city areas but
definitely not the small, one-horse towns, deserts,
and mountains.

His mind wandered to Maddie as he pushed
himself towards his fiftieth push-up. She was a
firecracker and rocked his world. Her zombie
slashing skills were a huge turn-on. It was as though
she was fearless but he knew better. She hated them
and, like everybody else, had sympathy for the now
dregs of society. It wasn't their fault. A flash of
golden hair swung in front of his mind's eye and
Maddie's blood-covered black nightgown.

It was their dream that guided them towards
each other. Far more than a coincidence, he thought,

but lacked a working theory. There was no more explanation for it than anything else. It frustrated him and pushed his motivation as he counted 150 push-ups. His arms growing weak, he worked through it, forcing 161.

Lifting off the floor, he stood, gazing at the endless sparkling water. For days that's all they'd seen and he could understand how people suffered cabin fever after being stuck on a boat for months at a time. He lifted a glass of juice to his lips and gulped a large swig. At the end of the glass something white bobbed on the water.

Dropping the glass into the cup holder he lifted the goggles to his eyes. *Was he actually seeing something or was it a mirage on the ocean?* The possibility was his mind wanted to see something, yet he wasn't so sure he actually did.

Even with the goggles he couldn't see much, but he was sure something was there. He sprinted out of the bridge and gauged the highest point on the boat then hung the goggles over his neck and climbed. When he reached the top he thrust them over his eyes once again. His mouth dropped as the white dot turned into a floating object resembling a boat.

It was their rule that if either spotted something on the water or anything that might be trouble they'd wake the other up, so Bryce wasted no time in sprinting to Jack's room and pushing his hand against his back, cutting off the man's snoring as he jolted upwards in bed.

Jack lurched out of bed as if it was on fire and scrambled to yank his pants on. "What's going on?"

Bryce's eyes were wide with a foreboding expression. "Several miles north. Something is drifting out there."

Jack rushed out of the cabin, not wasting time to pull on a shirt, and together they rushed to the bridge. Now close enough it could be seen more clearly from that point. He lifted the binoculars. "Looks like some kind of fishing boat. I say we get on board and take a look."

Bryce cringed at the thought. He really hated killing deaders but there was always a chance someone was alive on there and needed help. He double cringed at caring so much. *Why couldn't he shut his emotions off?*

It didn't take long before they were face to face with a fishing boat that appeared abandoned. Bryce steered and Jack lay across the sleek top of the yacht with the sniper rifle to his eye as he scanned. Movement inside the cabin caught his eye. He held the rifle and, as they drew close enough, realized what was in there wasn't living but deader.

From his spot he fired a bullet. It hit the cabin slightly to the side of his target. He'd fired too early. Adjusting the sight, he fired again. From this close he hoped the bullet would hit the glass with enough force to blow a hole in it and the head of the deader.

To his satisfaction, the deader dropped. Bryce slowed the yacht down and coasted to the side but not too close. The sound ringing from the shot and the deader's drop onto the floor of the cabin alerted more and within minutes movement swarmed the cabin.

Jack slid off the rounded surface of the boat and rushed inside. Bryce held a rifle in his hands. "You steer. I'll shoot." He caught the door from Jack's hand and not giving him time to complain he rushed onto the deck.

The deaders were trapped inside the cabin. Not intelligent enough to open the door, they snarled and gritted their teeth as they walked into the wall of the cabin. Their noses rising in the air as they smelled living flesh. Bryce shot through the glass and dropped two as they were standing one against the next. He fired again and dropped two more, then two more, until only a couple were left.

He moved around the yacht and angled the rifle to get a side shot at one bumping into the wall. He watched it shuffling forwards then shifting backwards from the force of the wall. Gauging it for a couple minutes he fired one off as it shifted backwards. Plugging it a hair above its ear, it fell.

Another moved towards the window. Its nose high in the air. "I smell you too and you stink like rotting trash," Bryce whispered to the air as he fired the rifle. It dropped like a chunk of lead. Scanning the cabin and deck he didn't spot anymore and returned to the bridge.

"That's fine shootin'!" Jack announced, steering the yacht around the fishing boat.

"Thanks, I'm going on board." Bryce didn't give Jack an option. He needed him at the helm and if anymore deaders were on the fishing boat he could handle it.

Jack nodded as he pulled the yacht as close as possible to the fishing boat. Bryce leveled a plank across the sides of the boats and grabbed the shovel and a handgun, tucking it into his waist. It would be tricky moving from one vessel to the next but he wasn't going to be zombie shark bait today. Determined, he didn't give himself the chance to rethink it. The fishing boat might have supplies and gas on board that would be of use to them.

Chapter Sixteen

Bryce pushed up from his feet with pride in his accomplishment. It hadn't been easy and required his athletic ability to get from one boat onto the next. Jack held the yacht's speed and Bryce loaded his shovel first onto the fishing boat, as climbing with it would pose too big a problem and serve to be a hindrance.

They hadn't seen any movement on deck so he chanced it. Gripping his shovel, he moved around the boat. A foul odor from the several dead zombies plunged into his nose and he attempted to breathe in and out of his mouth to avoid it.

A large, built-in cooler harbored several fish, still moving in the shallow water. They'd surely die. He searched the deck and found a net; using it he scooped the fish and tossed them into the ocean. Someone else may have kept them for consumption but since they didn't know how the virus affected animals and fish he wasn't risking it. His face twisted into a scowl as he thought about it.

The zombie shark and rat meant mammals and fish were not immune as they'd previously thought. The wriggling fish he tossed back into the Atlantic appeared unharmed but it wasn't worth the risk. The last one hitting the water with a splash, he closed the lid and opened his ears.

He didn't hear anything except the splash from the ocean as the boat rocked. He strode towards the helm, being careful to walk between the deaders.

Even though dead dead, it gave him an eerie vibe as he stepped between one and then the next.

Blowing out a breath, then lifting his T-shirt over his nose since breathing out of his mouth was proving a challenge, he pushed the cabin door open. Zombies lay in a pile, a messy pile, and their dark blood coated the walls. With his shovel he poked at them and when none moved he was sure that whatever amount of life they'd had was gone for good.

It hurt his heart to think about it and reeled his mind back to his father's face as he'd come at him shouting We-yak which they now knew stood for *Wetland Environment and Conservation.* The group his father was working with. Somehow they were responsible for making humanity a mess of walking dead. In Bryce's mind he saw his father's dead eyes as he closed him into the room and shoved the chair up to the knob. *Was he gone?*

It really wasn't a question. He was one of them, and Bryce only hoped the military had put him out of his misery. The idea of his father being a zombie brought tears to his eyes. He wiped them away and sucked back his sadness, hiding it in the corner of his mind, and took the steps leading to the sleeping quarters and galley below.

He searched each room, pushing the closed doors open with his shovel and carefully maneuvering into the open rooms. The silence on the boat was as eerie and dead as the zombies strewn about. He placed his hand on the final door and lowered his ear to it. Met with more silence, he

116

twisted the knob and stood back, shoving it open with his shovel. A man lay across a bed.

Chunks of flesh were missing from his legs and arms. His color pasty, his chest still, and his body horribly bloated, smelly, and out of proportion. Bryce knew he was dead. Not a deader but dead. The only person onboard immune to the disease and he was gone. Killed by the zombies and, possibly, starvation.

Bryce closed each door behind him, not that it made the stench any less but it made him feel better as prickles rose and fell on his legs and arms. The nightmare on this boat worse than a scene in any horror movie.

He went another level down to the engine room, listened at the door. Hearing tiny scratches he pushed the door open and scanned the room. Sets of tiny beady eyes glowed from beneath equipment. More zombie rats. He slammed the door shut and stepped backwards. His back hitting something round and firm. The barrel of a gun.

Chapter Seventeen

"Raise them arms," said a deep, booming voice.

Bryce elevated his arms above his head, the gun still in his hand, which the man removed promptly.

"I should thank you for cleaning up this mess. Once everyone turned it got ugly. That boat you got is real nice. Someone else gotta be on it. You might as well tell me now." His words slurred together but Bryce heard him clearly.

The shovel leaned against the space where the door frame met the wall. The man's intentions didn't feel right; not only the gun to his back but the slur of his words. Bryce considered going for it but questioned if he'd be quick enough. Instead he turned around slowly.

"Stop it right there!"

Bryce halted. The man meant business and he wasn't going to risk it but wait for a better opportunity. "My family's onboard the other boat. We're running out of supplies..."

The man pushed the barrel further into Bryce's back, right on the spinal cord. He recoiled slightly from the pain but not enough the man took any notice. *How did I miss him?* he wondered, his mind replaying every step he'd taken since climbing onboard and couldn't think of anything he missed, except maybe... the bedroom of the dead, uninfected guy. He hadn't gone further than to peer inside. That had to be it.

The man's deep voice and cowboy mannerisms so far gave him the feel of a tough guy. Or one that thought he was but hiding with a dead guy instead of offing the zombies wasn't too brave or heroic. He'd give him the belief he was in need. "My family's on that boat. We could use another gun."

The man coughed. "What makes you think I want to help you?"

Bryce stuttered on purpose, "I thought... um... well. We could...a…"

"Spit it out!" The man's words strangled in his cough.

Bryce eyes shifted again to the shovel as the man gagged and choked. The gun still square against his back. "You don't sound so good. We can help you."

Breathless, the man's words caught in his throat as he spit them out. "Don't... need... it... this... will... pass."

Thump, thump sounded through the man's strangled coughing fit. He tuned his ears into the thumping -- footsteps. *Did he leave a deader alive? Surely Jack would have seen someone else if they'd attempted to board the vessel?* Anger and fear swirled together. *Was Jack still in control of the yacht?* Without a second thought, his life in the balance, he grabbed the shovel and spun his body around. The man's hand dropped, his body against the wall, torso lowered with his vacant hand over his mouth.

Bryce lifted the shovel and drove it hard onto the top of the man's head. He dropped to the floor

on his knees and Bryce shoved the pointed end
below his hairline into his neck. Blood poured from
the wound as Bryce pulled the end out. The man
dropped to the side and Bryce kicked him over.
Greyish blue skin covered his shirtless chest and
arms. His face the same sickly color.

"Wondered what was taking so long. You
done?"

Bryce jumped backwards as he lifted his eyes to
the voice. Even though he immediately recognized
it, the sound still startled him. "The yacht Jack.
You've left it unguarded!" As soon as the words left
his mouth he knew he shouldn't have said it. If it
wasn't for the man's unrelenting hack he'd remain
stuck here with a gun barrel cozied to his back from
the unstable captor.

Swishing a toothpick from one side of his mouth
to the other, Jack shrugged then turned on his heel
and stomped back up the steps.

Bryce blew out a breath. Jack knew boats and
would have secured everything properly before
hopping ship. He'd apologize later; for now he
wanted to inspect this man further. Unlacing the
man's boots and tugging them off, he tossed them to
the side. An odor almost as obnoxious as the
zombies hit him hard and fast in the nose. He
flinched for a second then regained control and
wrenched at the man's socks that were brown with
dirt and glued to his feet from grime.

A few moments later he had the man stripped
down to his birthday suit. No signs of any bites,
scratches, or anything that would give him a reason

to be infected. Bryce lowered himself and more closely inspected the man, even pulled off his skid-marked underwear. His body wasn't flawless by any means and carried a number of scars, but no evidence of a bite.

He grabbed his shovel and gun, tucking the gun into his waistband, closed his eyes, opened them and entered the dead nondeader man's room. His nose adjusting to the ghastly odor, he noted a large lidded bowl in the corner of the room. He lifted the lid and gawked. A half-eaten fish along with a litter of fish bones was inside. He closed the lid.

The man had been subsisting on fish they'd caught. *How did he get to the fish without becoming zombie food or bitten?* He'd never know and wasn't wasting any more time on it. What the discovery did prove was more important. No animal was safe to eat without getting ill. That also answered how the shark and rat got ill. They'd eaten zombie flesh.

The shark, rat, and man were much quicker. The man even talked and displayed reasoning skills. He hadn't known he was turning zombie until he looked at him. Somehow the virus affected animals differently when they ate meat rather than were infected by other means. *Did that mean it was mutating?*

He took the stairs two at a time. Once he cleared the lower floor and scrambled onto the deck he remembered his hasty words toward Jack. Rotating his neck he peered toward the yacht and let out a breath of relief when it was still there.

Chapter Eighteen

They coasted the yacht into a port off Virginia Beach, using gas fumes, choosing to hoof it or hotwire a vehicle to stay under the Navy's radar. Once anchored, they loaded the boat with gas, noting no movement, and gathered their weapons and supplies. Neither saw any zombies but they weren't leaving anything to chance.

Stalking silently, heel to toe, they managed to make it to the parking lot without a single deader appearance. It was a hike to get close enough to the naval base in order to spy even with the binoculars. Bryce wondered how Maddie and her family were getting along and hoped their travels were safe. He felt the thin outline of his cell phone in his pocket. It was fully charged but wouldn't do him any good unless he wanted to be found. It gave him a certain security as a last ditch effort of communication with them if everything went sour.

The sun shone bright against the pavement and he was glad he wore sunglasses and pulled his long hair back. Sweat beaded on Jack's forehead and neck. The humidity in Virginia was nearly as bad as Florida, but a light ocean breeze made it bearable. They found a parking lot with only a few cars. Bryce wasn't sure if that should worry him or not. Guns at the ready, they peered into the vehicles.

No deaders present but he expected they'd see piles left from the military when they reached the streets. He smelled the stench of death strong in the air surrounding them like a rotten egg sandwich.

Jack found a large Ford truck, doors unlocked, keys beneath the visor. The diesel engine fired up and rumbled surprisingly quietly as they cruised out of the parking lot, making along highway 64 and around the base. As they'd expected, deaders were piled up similar to what they'd seen in Morocco before leaving. Neither man understood why they piled them instead of destroying them, unless there were simply too many.

The zombie bodies were at varying stages of decomposition. Some were bloated, others had layers of skin falling off their faces and exposed areas on their arms, chests, and legs. Jack rolled the truck through the havoc that was the freeway, dodging stopped cars, doors open as if the occupants had been dragged from them. The bodies littered the shoulder. Finally he rolled the truck to a stop a distance across the bay from the base. He figured they might as well knock on their front door and announce their presence if they got any closer.

Rumbling overhead alerted Jack and Bryce to the military's presence. They stayed inside the truck until the source of rumbling helicopters passed overhead and moved away from them, dropping out of sight at the naval air station.

Once the whirring and rumbling vanished, positive the copters had landed, they stepped out of the truck and, keeping low, stalked through the streets of a housing development. It unnerved Bryce as he thought of this place filled with people mowing lawns that were now grown out of control and manicuring their trees.

When they reached Chesapeake Ave they ducked beneath a thick, wide clump of bushes, the sandy shores of the beach below them. Through binoculars, they watched. The port was visible but they couldn't see the air station. A few ships were docked, following the teams of soldiers on their way somewhere.

They watched them board a carrier similar in style to the USS America. It was compact, with a landing deck filled with helicopters.

Jack's voice low, the binoculars still pasted to his eyes, he said, "Looks like they're readying for another mission. That's the USS Wasp an LHD-1. First in its class."

Bryce shifted his eyes in the binoculars and scanned the area, noticing something out of place, or at least he thought. It blended into the surrounding environment but the glare from the sun is what caught his eye. It shone just above the treetops and he realized the base was surrounded by a casing similar to a green house. It stopped on the outer edges of the roadway that wrapped the ports.

Bryce's brain turned faster than the wheels of a runaway truck. He nudged Jack. "The whole place is surrounded in a type of dome, like the zombie sickness is some type of environmental disaster. It protects the inhabitants from the outside contaminated air. The same air we're breathing." As the words left his tongue he finally got it. "That's why they haven't destroyed the bodies. It would spread the illness to any survivors outside the bubble."

The son of an environmental scientist, he knew a thing or two about protecting it and the organisms that resided in it. No doubt in his mind the illness was airborne, which would explain how it spread so quickly.

Jack clucked his tongue, finding the dome and considering Bryce's words. "I reckon you're right. That's why they're wearing those masks, not everyone is immune like us. They're collecting everyone alive and bringin' them here so's they don't get sick. They might even be testing the immune ones to find out what makes them immune. Heck, I wonder how many facilities they got like this around the world."

Bryce's thinking worked quicker than Jack's and beyond any doubt the military and the U.S. government had known about this illness for a while, long enough to secure this base and make a plan of action. "I'm sure there are others. Probably at least one on the west coast in San Diego. What gets me is they had the time to prepare, meaning they've known about this for some time."

As if that thought hadn't occurred to Jack, he dropped his binoculars. "You got somethin' there boy. Maybe this illness was an act from the government to lessen the world's growing population. You know, weed out the people so we don't get overcrowded."

Bryce raised a brow. He wouldn't go that far, but obviously the government knew something and kept it from the populace.

If they could get to the port, which wasn't beneath the dome but was across the Chesapeake from them maybe they could find a way in. Swimming all that way wasn't an option and a boat would be seen by the many MPs with their M-16 rifles. Jack scratched his bald head, deep in thought. There had to be a way in but it wasn't portside.

The ship left with a full military crew on board. Bryce and Jack loaded back into the truck and onto the freeway, taking the long way around the base. They'd had to take a bridge there and followed the same bridge back. There were two, but this one had more distance from the base and the guards. Bryce continued to pan the binoculars over the area. People moved around inside the dome as if it was a normal day. Jack rolled the truck to a stop and they climbed out. From their vantage point they saw the air station. It had its own dome inside the larger dome. Lying with their bellies on the ground, they army-crawled as close as they could safely get without being spotted.

The familiar whirring of blades cutting through the atmosphere and blowing the air surrounding them. Beneath a grouping of trees, Jack was pretty sure they hadn't been made. The dome pushed back like a trash can lid and the copters lowered into place.

Soldiers jumped out of the copters with civilians; children, adults -- young and old; about a dozen and a half was Bryce's count.

It was late into the afternoon and the sun was setting on the horizon, spreading an array of colors over the sky. "I reckon we hole up in one of these homes for the night," Jack suggested. "We'll get a fresh start in the morning." He stood and dusted off his clothing.

They had their choice of homes, all were vacant. They chose one in the middle of a cul-de-sac to get as far away from the rotting zombies as they could. Inside the house with the doors closed the odor of death was minimal.

Bryce opened his pack and took out a can of fruit and a few strips of beef jerky. He handed a couple strips to Jack.

Sinking his teeth into the jerky, Jack yanked a chunk off. Talking with a mouthful he said, "Tomorrow we should separate and check out the rest of the base."

Bryce swallowed his chunk of jerky. "Should we go back out there tonight? They can't see us easily in the dark."

About to take a bite, Jack lowered his hand from his mouth. "I'm not sure we should do that."

Bryce couldn't imagine why. Their best cover was night and from what they'd seen not a living soul survived outside the dome here. "I think we should."

Jack squinted an eye. "They have night vision. They'll see our heat signatures. If we aren't careful they'll spot us. It's been a long day and we'll be more prone to mistakes."

Understanding his point of view, Bryce finished his meal of beef jerky and mixed fruit then took to the couch.

A low rumble startled Bryce out of his sleep. He glanced to the chair where Jack lay snoring, sucking air in and blowing it out with a familiar reverberation. He'd found his snore annoying in the beginning but now found it comforting to know someone was near and alive. He crawled to the window and glimpsed out, searching for the source.

Maybe thunder. Then it started again and continued moving in their direction. A car; it was definitely a car. They needed to hide. He remembered Jack's warning about night vision. His mouth curled. He knew night vision worked off infrared or heat signatures. How could he hide them?

In the movies they covered themselves in mud but that wasn't an option. A cold bath, but there probably wasn't any water, cold or hot. Metal, during an x-ray they covered exposed areas with lead. Infrared was lower on the spectrum and wouldn't need something as heavy as lead. Jumping to his feet he ran to the kitchen and shifted through the cabinets, tossing everything onto the floor until he found it - aluminum foil.

"Jack, Jack," he whispered pushing his hand against his back.

Jack shot up, stared Bryce in the eye, his own eyes wide. "What?"

"Something's coming. Stand up so I can wrap you."

Jack's brows shot upwards and he scratched his cheek.

"This should block their night vision," Bryce said as he wrapped Jack's torso, arms, and legs.

The rumble continued in their direction, low and steady, as Jack wrapped Bryce. They hunkered beneath a window, aluminum covering their bodies. Their breathing heavy as they waited for it to pass.

Muffled voices outside grabbed their attention. "Probably a dog or something."

"Noah called it in. He's always spot on."

"I don't see anything. No movement. There's nothing here."

Jack sat and worked at slowing his breathing. He didn't know if aluminum foil would actually work but gave Bryce the benefit of the doubt. He was a clever kid.

A flashlight shone through the window above their heads. Pulling their legs in, backs against the wall, Bryce and Jack sat still as mannequins. The glow moved around the room, dispersing light in a cone. It swept the floor then it was gone.

Chapter Nineteen

When the sun came up the next day, Bryce and Jack watched the helicopters whir into the air. Plastering themselves against the ground for camouflage, they lay still, heads to the ground. The aluminum had worked; effectively masking their signatures. He would remember that and keep a spare with him at all times in the pack he'd found on the yacht. It was his survival kit. The copter blades blew the plant life around them and the whirring sliced through the air, blasting their eardrums. From the sound, the copters went off in various directions.

After several minutes Bryce lifted his head. Noting the helicopters were gone, he sat up and stared through the binoculars, observing them. Jack followed suit and they concocted a plan. The dome was thick and military milled around inside it. They stalked closer and stayed low. MPs wearing masks were posted outside the dome with M-16s at their side.

Bryce and Jack, using their binoculars, swept the inside of the dome which in Jack's opinion was business as usual, nothing strange going on even though the entire situation was peculiar. They separated in order to cover the entire radius of the dome and would meet back at their departing location. They set their radios to a different frequency than the military to stay in touch.

Bryce crept through the brush, crouch-walking to stay out of sight. He didn't want the guards posted high in the dome to take notice of his movement. The base was huge and they wouldn't be able to reach the sides surrounded by water. Propping the binoculars back over his eyes, he scanned the area. People, dressed in civilian clothes, were out and about in what appeared to be a housing sector. Rows of homes lined the streets as people milled about.

The uncertainty he'd felt in Morocco watching the survivors forced to board the carrier, some willing, some not, eased. These people weren't prisoners but brought to safety, kept in a world free of the illness turning people into walking dead machines whose only function was eating -- devouring other living souls.

For a long moment he watched and considered. Somehow they needed to get inside, but also assurance they'd be able to leave. The dome had a retractable roof over the air station and the gate allowing the sailors to the port but there was also a ground level exit not far from the air station. All were secure but the back exit wasn't guarded as tightly as the portside. It might be their only chance of getting in. They needed a plan, a good one.

In the dome was a farm including chickens, roosters, turkeys, and cows. He'd also seen what looked like a training camp filled with young adults no older than Bryce. Unease settled into his belly. *Were they collecting the immune to build an army out of them?*

Bryce shrugged. It was better than testing. At this point neither could say whether they were testing anyone or not or even if all those people were immune. From what they'd seen it didn't appear so, but they had to have medical staff at the hospital. His mind was more focused on getting into and out of the base. It was impenetrable.

By the time Bryce and Jack met back up the sun was lowering beneath the horizon, leaving the land dark. Heavy winds from the east kicked up and the sky rumbled. Lights blinked from poles outside the dome, brightening the area. A rustle from the brush behind them caught their attention. No sooner had they turned their heads than the barrel of an M-16 stared at them.

Through the mask, the soldier ordered, his voice unforgiving, "Stand up, hands above your heads." His voice carried a southern U.S. accent and his uniform was clearly Army fatigues.

Neither Bryce nor Jack was in a position to argue, not with the machine gun pointed at their heads. They stood and kept their hands up above their heads as ordered. The ground litter crunched beneath the weight of their feet. Standing tall, hands raised, they stood side by side, not more than an inch between them and stared wide-eyed at the soldier with the gun. Neither said a word.

The soldier shifted the gun downward and ran it the length of them, poising it once again at their heads. "How'd you git out here?"

They glanced at each other, confused by his question. Jack lowered one lid in a half-wink at Bryce as if he had some kind of plan. He wasn't always the brightest but knew a thing or two, so Bryce let him take the lead.

Clearing his voice Jack began, "We didn't git out here. We've been out here."

That wasn't what Bryce was hoping for so he nudged him lightly. It might be better to play the game, he thought, than allow the military to know they hadn't captured every U.S. living -- as in not zombie -- alive person in the country. That is if they'd combed the U.S. It was a large country and had many secluded areas.

The soldier eyed Jack through the clear lenses of the mask. He looked like an alien with the thing protruding from his mouth. "What do you mean?"

Jack pushed an elbow into Bryce, clueing him that he had this under control. Bryce wasn't so sure but let him continue. The end game was getting into the facility.

"The Cranberry Wilderness. Got a cabin up there. My boy here and I, we like livin' in the quiet, secluded from the city, surviving off the land. We don't leave often and when we did we seen the bodies piled up. Why don't you tell us what's going on?" Jack worked his best country accent.

The man shifted the gun as if holding it towards their faces was tiring his arms. "Walk," the soldier ordered.

Jack stood his ground, placing an arm over Bryce's chest as if protecting him from something. "Dead people are everywhere. You have a gun to our faces and you think we should just go with you. I don't think so."

The soldier poked the gun at his chest. "Move!"

In a swift movement, quicker than a jet, Jack had control of the soldier's weapon and thrust it against the side of his head, knocking him against the skull. He dropped.

Jack placed the gun on the ground. "Quick, we need to get this uniform off him before someone notices he's left his post."

Bryce shook his head as if he hadn't seen Jack take out the soldier. It was an impressive move. "How did you do that?"

Jack chuckled as he tugged the man's boots off. "A trick my ex-wife taught me. She was a self-defense instructor." Dropping the soldier's second boot to the side, Jack tugged at his pants while Bryce pulled at his shirt then stopped.

Married? Bryce guessed there was still a lot they didn't know about each other. The camouflage shirt and jacket pulled over the soldier's chest, Bryce thought twice about taking it off. What if the air was contaminated and the soldier would turn into a zombie once he inhaled it. He couldn't be responsible for that.

"Take it off." Jack tugged at the soldier's gas mask.

Bryce grabbed Jack's wrists. "We can't. We might kill him if we do."

Jack poised his fingers against his forehead and rubbed. "You may be right. We can't take that chance." He dragged his hand over his face and tugged at his chin. "I got a plan."

A few minutes later they had the soldier dressed again and Bryce lay against the earth. Jack covered him in ground litter then dragged the soldier, an arm over his shoulder, toward the dome exit.

Eyes on Jack and the soldier, Bryce lay still. The M-16 and their other weapons with him, except the rifle Jack favored. Alone, he noted there were no crickets chirping. Large water droplets fell from the sky and lightning shot across it, lighting up the area.

The soldier's feet dragged the ground, leaving a trail in the mud as they neared the dome and a swarm of soldiers banded together inside the safety of the bubble. Jack halted and two outside guards moved towards him.

"Hands up!" an MP, six feet or more in height and thin, called to Jack.

"If I do this man will fall," replied Jack.

A shorter soldier moved towards Jack as the taller one hung back. "Drop him carefully." The high-pitched, rigid voice was that of a woman.

Jack lowered the soldier to the ground with care. The rifle still in hand.

The female soldier kept her M-16 poised on him. "Stand up, back straight, and hand me the weapon."

She didn't appear large enough to hold two heavy weapons but looks could be deceiving. "I found your man about fifty yards out," he said, attempting to keep his voice steady. Like a drummer after drinking several energy drinks, his heart beat in his chest. He'd never been much of a liar.

Squawk, beep, went a radio. "Found a live one, not infected," said the female soldier, the radio even with the tip of her chin.

Static gripped the air and Jack's insides. Torrents of water rushed over his face and their helmets and gas masks as several soldiers moved through the dome exit. Two collected the soldier and another grabbed Jack's wrists and banded them against his back like he was a prisoner.

"Bring him to the gate," a disembodied voice blasted over the radio.

Soon the gate opened and Jack was forced inside. He did his best to take his mind off the situation. Staying calm and in control was imperative and, by-golly, it was the military. The U.S. military, all branches by the looks and sounds of it. He could trust them... or could he?

Rivulets of water poured over the dome and trickled over the sides and more lightning bolted from the sky. Bryce was a smart kid; he was sure he'd taken cover. The way they escorted him roughly into the dome didn't send any warm fuzzies down his spine.

"Careful! What's going on and is this how you treat everyone?!" He said all that mostly to get his mind off the possibility they'd made a mistake and getting into the dome wasn't the brightest idea. Swallowing his fear, he stayed in step with the MPs.

Chapter Twenty

Bryce

It had been three days and no sign of Jack. He watched daily and kept the radio set to the military's frequency. In Norfolk, he found a hotel empty of deaders and shacked up in one of the rooms. It wasn't far from the base. He gazed out the window and couldn't help but wonder how they'd cleansed the entire city. There were at least twenty floors in the hotel. He was on the second floor and had walked its length and counted sixteen rooms. Downstairs was a conference room, gym, shops, restaurant and bar; taking that into account he figured the hotel had at least 150 rooms. The military was efficient.

From his second story window he watched the copters pass overhead and veer off in various patterns, searching for survivors, he figured. Gearing up, he headed out. He'd considered leaving some gear in the truck since he hadn't seen anything alive outside the dome but decided there was a large enough chance more renegades like him were around and staying low key. He kept the truck in a garage so it was out of sight. Hopping in, he started the motor and pulled onto the street.

Today he planned on getting to the other side of the Chesapeake to try and get a look at the Naval Port. He'd found a map at the gas station he'd used to fill up the previous night. He marked the route in red. He followed the roads and parked in the middle of the road so the truck blended with the other vehicles abandoned after the apocalypse hit. He walked a distance before he came to an area that overlooked the bay and the base. Without the binoculars he couldn't see much, but with them he had a decent view of the port.

A ship, the name he couldn't see but it was larger than the USS America, was being loaded and prepped as soldiers made signals and hauled bags on board, moving inside. A crew outside directed the flow. The masks over their heads, he couldn't see any faces. Within the hour the ship started out. He ducked low beneath the thick brush to keep himself hidden.

Portside appeared more heavily guarded than the back exit, but if he could get to a port he might be able to sneak in.

Jack

After drawing a vial of blood, fingerprinting him, and asking a series of questions, Jack was taken to a light blue room absent of windows and left alone. It wasn't until a couple hours later that he was joined by a commander and a couple of low rank officers.

The commander's thin lips stretched in a straight line across his poker face. "Jack Glenny, retired Coast Guard." He tugged at his ginger beard. "I thought to myself what hick would bring a soldier to our gate, but you're no hick. Your last address is

Jacksonville, Florida. The story you fed my guy won't fly with me."

Jack considered his options. He could be honest, but couldn't begin to explain the adventure he'd survived the past several weeks of his life and he knew nobody in his group wanted to be found. He could lie; that would be easier. "I did live in Jacksonville. When those dead things took over I loaded up and headed north to the mountains."

The commander pushed his lips out. "And what about the boy?"

Jack had forgotten the MP had seen Bryce and no doubt told all about his encounter. "I picked him up along the way."

"Where is he?"

Jack shrugged. "He could be anywhere."

The commander handed him the radio he'd had on him when they'd brought him on base. "Why don't you contact him?"

Taking the radio he clutched it in his hand, narrowed his eyes as he stared hard into the commander's. An assortment of ideas about what he should say ran through his head. He truly didn't know, his mind drawing blanks. He pressed the button and it beeped then released it slowly. "Milligan," he called then pressed the button again. No response. He let out a breath, relieved Bryce hadn't responded.

Milligan was his grandfather's name and the first one that came to mind. He attempted a couple more times, adjusting the frequency -- nothing. The commander bought the ruse.

"Take the radio," the commander ordered to a young Petty Officer. The private did as he was told and the commander glared Jack in the eye. If looks could kill he'd be dead. "Leave us," he ordered, waving the low level soldiers out of the room.

His eyes turned again to Jack. "You're coming with me."

Confused and stifling his fear, Jack stood and followed the commander into the hallway and outside the building. Soldiers joked and everything was about as normal as he'd seen in any military installment. The commander hopped onto the seat of a golf cart and urged Jack to ride shot gun. It wasn't that he really had a choice.

They drove around the base, through the work areas. "This is the most secure location on the East Coast. The dome around us keeps the zombies and whatever diseases they're carrying out. We check everyone we let in. All we need is a sample of blood to rule out the illness. Your blood showed something few of our soldiers do. Your blood forms antibodies against the disease." The cart rolled to a stop at the sign beneath a bushy tree. He checked both ways then proceeded forward.

Jack stayed quiet, his mind attempting to process and understand what the commander was getting at. He figured he was immune or something since he hadn't gotten sick and the commander had to have known too since he wasn't ill or showing any signs.

The commander cleared his throat. "We need people who can't get sick out there on the boats, rescuing others and bringing them back here."

Jack lowered his brows. "You want me on a boat?"

The commander smiled. "The boy -- he's immune too?"

Jack nodded.

"We need him, too. We need everyone we can get." He rolled the cart to a stop. In front of them was a group, all ages from about fifteen to forty going through training. He recognized the drills from his military days. "The sickness has affected the entire globe. We bring them in, feed them, house them and their families -- those that haven't lost their loved ones to the sickness. Once they understand they're safe we ask them to join. The ones like you, their blood builds antibodies against the disease. You're an even bigger commodity because you know how to sail."

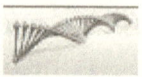

The commander's words weighed heavily on his mind as he lay on the bed in the small barracks room they'd given him. It didn't have much, but the bed wasn't too uncomfortable and the walls weren't that anxiety causing shade of blue in the first room. He could come and go. Lifting up, he sauntered out of the building, soldiers passing him here and there.

Twilight was approaching and he weighed whether he should get grub at the mess hall or continue. He was given a sandwich earlier and his stomach wasn't grumbling, so he continued towards base housing. He still had so many questions that rose to the front of his mind while he walked the streets at a healthy pace. First on his mind was what was an antibody? He should know the answer but he didn't. Did it mean he was immune? If his body responded by making something then he wasn't immune but had a natural defense against the disease. Yeah, that was it. His good old blood cells hard at work. Arriving at the first set of apartment buildings he marched forward in his civilian clothes.

An older woman sat to the side of a building on a bench and two small children scampered across a playground. A couple older children played hopscotch in the setting sun down a couple blocks. All he saw were older adults and young children. Teenagers and young adults were absent, probably in training to be part of the "new" military.

He thought of the commander's proposal. It stuck in his mind and attached itself like superglue. His mission started as purely surviving, then grew into something more after hooking up with Maddie, Bryce, and their families. Protecting the group became paramount. Now he was seriously thinking about assisting in the salvation of all living people in the world. A global catastrophic event that out did any volcano, hurricane, or even tsunami.

He wished there was some way to contact Bryce. *Where was he?* Jack decided in order to finish the mission he and Bryce set out to do, he first needed a walkie-talkie and answers to his questions. All the soldiers had radios. It might not be that much of a challenge to contact Bryce he realized as he stared at a radio left on the bathroom counter.

It was a community bathroom so he grabbed it searching for the soldier to whom the radio belonged. Not seeing anyone, he pushed the radio into his pants and scurried back to his room. When he reached the door he thought twice as they may have cameras about and decided to take another stroll outside.

Rounding the barracks he almost bumped into a captain but excused himself, saluted, and was dismissed. One hundred feet or so from the barracks was a patch of trees. He'd use them for cover. Pushing through the bushes surrounding the trees, he crouched and turned the dial of the radio to the frequency he and Bryce used. "Bryce," he spoke into it.

No response. "Bryce. It's Jack."

Still no response. He wasn't about to give up. Maybe Bryce changed the frequency in order to listen in on others. *There had to be more people out there, right?* he thought to himself and tried a couple other frequencies.

Finally, a voice talked back. "Jack."

"It's good to hear you. I don't have much time. The commander wants me to run missions because of my Coast Guard training and... and my, my antibodies."

The radio fell silent and Jack thought he'd lost him then the familiar squawk hit his ears. "Did you learn anything else?"

Jack was more than a little disappointed that he ignored his message. "No, nothing."

"Rescue missions?"

"Yes, they bring them here and the young adults they put into training to get them out on missions. The ones like me with antibodies," Jack responded. He was really hoping Bryce would tell him about antibodies but he didn't want to directly ask him. He'd feel stupid.

The radio was silent again for a long pause. "Is this what you want?"

"No, not really, but maybe it's something I need to do, help save others like ourselves." He didn't hide the apprehension in his voice. The idea unnerved him but, as a former soldier, he easily understood the commander's request.

"10-4."

Jack lowered his voice, "Will contact you later. Keep this frequency open." He switched the radio off and tucked it into the center of a large bush, tossing the available leaf clutter over it and peered over the top. The coast was clear so he left.

Chapter Twenty-One

The following morning, after a sleepless night of tossing and turning, he marched into the commander's office. He knew proper etiquette but didn't care. If he wanted him on a boat assisting than he owed him some answers.

The commander's chair was swiveled toward the window. He didn't even turn around before addressing him, "Jack. I take it you've thought about my proposal."

Lowering himself into the plush chair across from the bulky wooden desk Jack said, "I have and I have a few answers I need first."

The commander swiveled around then. The slightest amount of stubble coated his chin and cheeks as if he hadn't shaved that morning. "What is it you'd like to know?"

Jack sucked in a large breath to keep calm. Never in his Coast Guard career would he have ever barged into the office of anyone of this man's rank and then not addressed him as 'Sir'. On top of that he was making demands. "How long did the government know about this sickness? This dome wasn't built overnight."

The commander swallowed and tented his hands under his chin. "A couple of years. That's how long it took to construct the enclosure and make this base self-sufficient."

"So they knew about it, everything." *And what the heck are antibodies?* He left that part out.

"Not everything. I'm a Captain not the President or Homeland Security but it was brought to my attention. I wasn't even the commander of this base when everything went down. I was just promoted to Captain and having been stationed here for a period of time during the construction I immediately brought my family here when the first reports made the news. Unfortunately, my family didn't make it. What you see here is all we have left of our forces on the east coast. San Diego is constructed much like this. The bases are self-sufficient with hydroponics for growing food and a small farm area for raising livestock. It's like Noah's Ark on land."

Jack stared him in the eye. "Do we have any government left?"

The commander chuckled. "You're looking at it. This is America and it's filled with those from the eastern side of the Mississippi to people from across the Atlantic. When I got here there was a skeleton crew. I made my own protocol. It's our job to save those unaffected."

"But what caused all this?"

"An environmental disaster. Most of the files were destroyed. A doomsday computer virus wiped most everything on base. We rebuilt from scratch using the highest technology in the country housed at this base and San Diego. You tell me, who knew?"

Jack gulped. The implications of what he said meant the government knew about it and most likely not just the U.S. but globally. All developed countries. He leaned back, his mind reeling. "The virus. That's what took the power out and cell phones."

The commander nodded his head. "You're starting to see the picture now, but our government had the foresight to prepare. They didn't have the immunity to live."

"If I bring in the boy, you have to give him free will to come and go. To make his own choices."

The commander nodded. "He's immune, like you. We have no desire to trap you or him in the facility. It is best practice to keep everyone under our thumb until we have found all the survivors and have more information on what caused this. We don't want the hundreds alive to die."

Bryce

In the same location as the previous day, Bryce watched the base. Another ship took the other one's place like a rotation. He didn't have any ideas how to get onto the base but felt relief to hear from Jack. They wanted immune people. He was immune, but did he want to assist on search and rescue missions?

Bryce strode back to his truck, his mind on Jack's words the previous day. *Did he want to join him?* He worried for Maddie and the others. He'd had no contact with them. The slim phone in his pocket a reminder. Pulling it out, unconcerned now if they found him, he turned it on. Within a few minutes the apps magically appeared.

He jerked his head when he heard voices. Two people stood beside his truck, doors open. He stepped back and raised his gun. Scanning his surroundings, he noted a silver Dodge with a flat tire. It hadn't been there before. He was sure of that. Taking a deep breath he brought the gun he carried upward and pointed it towards them.

His plan wasn't to harm anyone but protect himself and that was his truck. Jack had stolen it first and he had the keys in his pocket.

"Check this out. This truck is sweet!" called a dark curly-haired teen propped in the driver's seat. His wild hair looked as though it hadn't been brushed for days.

A taller one, a bit on the chunky side with a *Vikings* cap and a rifle strapped over his shoulder, said, "We could do some damage with that. Those things wouldn't stand a chance."

As he listened to their banter, he realized they weren't any older than him at the most, but they were armed. He waited, hoping they'd move on, plenty of other cars were parked in the street. Once the dark-haired one went beneath the seat, Bryce knew they weren't moving on. They had their sights set on his ride. Ducking back, he pressed the panic button. The alarm blared and the dark-haired one jumped out of the truck like a snake bit him.

"What the..." he shouted.

The other took several steps back, brought his rifle to his eyes and scanned the brush. Bryce lowered himself beneath the brush line, or so he thought, until the boy's eyes stopped, peering directly at him. "I see you. Drop any weapons."

Bryce dropped his gun but he still carried a hunting knife in his back pocket. He lifted his hands into the air.

"This your truck?"

He'd figured the alarm would freak them out and they'd move on. It was a sorry underestimation. The *Vikings,* a Minnesota team... was it possible they'd traveled that far? If so, they'd had plenty of their own battles and stories to tell.

Bryce walked forward, hands still in the air. "Yes, I don't want any trouble."

"Neither do we, but looks like we found it. Our car has a flat and without a spare, we need your truck," *Vikings* Hat said.

The other boy poised a 9 mm and walked around the other side of Bryce. Both moved closer.

"Toss us the keys!" the dark-haired one shouted.

Bryce pushed his hand into his pocket.

"Don't try anything," *Viking*s hat shouted.

Bryce pulled his hand out, keys curled in his finger. "Listen, I'm alone. We're all alive. I know you've seen them, even killed them."

"Not for a couple days. Seems they've died of hunger or something," said Dark Hair.

Obviously they weren't real bright or observant. *Hadn't they seen the helicopters?* "Listen, I know a safe place. I'll take you there."

Vikings Hat laughed. "There ain't no safe place and you won't be alive long if you don't toss those keys."

Bryce clutched the keys, preparing to toss them between the boys. His gun was only a couple steps away. At that moment the dust and dirt kicked up in their eyes followed by a rumble and a helicopter rose over head. Weapons still poised, Dark Hair and *Vikings* Hat shifted their eyes upwards.

"Drop the weapons boys," called an ominous voice from a loudspeaker.

A soldier leaned out the copter with a gun larger than theirs aimed at them. They quickly dropped their weapons.

Once it landed, Jack stepped out and walked towards Bryce. "When I didn't get a response from the radio we tracked your phone. What made you turn it on?"

Bryce's poker face gave nothing away as he stared Jack in the eye. "I didn't."

Jack's brows lowered and he ran his hand over his bald head. "Maybe it was the boys."

A smile erupted on Bryce's face. "It was me." He punched him in the shoulder. "I guess it was wishful thinking. Smart I did."

Jack rubbed the area. "You know I bruise." He grabbed Bryce and gave him a five second man-hug.

Vikings Hat and Dark Hair stood with their hands up, confused expressions on their faces.

"Looks like we got two more," the commander said as he walked near the boys. "You're coming with us." He cleared his throat and a soldier escorted them towards the waiting helicopter.

Chapter Twenty-Two

Maddie

Our final moments in Cape Town had been a close call. Bloody Mary had cut through the dead and the living that surrounded the airport. Their crude weapons were no match. As the vehicle plowed forward, the living jumped into their vehicles.

Mesi, Heather, myself, and Sarah took control of the side guns while Mazi kept the blades whirring from the driver's seat. We escaped the deaders.

Eshe had woken while we were gone and gave my parents his story, which was as crazy as ours. He was a simple bell hop on vacation to visit his family in the UK when the plane crashed in the mountains. He and the man with the thumb drive survived. Everybody else was dead, not even yet zombies. The man he traveled with didn't handle things so well and showed signs of illness, but he plugged along.

It was days of traveling with nothing when they finally came across their first deader. It ambled towards them and the man shot it between the eyes. It dropped on sight, spasming. The closer they got to civilization, the more deaders they came across, and the worse shape the man was in. It was at night while they were camping that a deader fell upon their makeshift camp site. Eshe was on guard, but had fallen asleep. He woke to the man's shouts as a deader bit into his cheek. With an unsteady hand

Eshe shot towards the deader and incidentally shot it
and the man. He'd never fired a gun before.

His instinct was to run, but he thought twice and
helped the man from under the deader, who he'd
luckily shot in the head. The man wasn't so lucky.
His bullet wound was in his neck and he bled out
profusely. Within a short amount of time, he passed.
Eshe, being an idiot who never watched a zombie
movie or show in his life, attempted to save the man
but it was a losing battle. Instead of shooting his
dying body in the head to put him out of his misery,
he rummaged through what belongings the man had
with him.

He'd remembered the man mentioned
something along their travels about a drive
containing important information about world
security. He also needed more bullets in case he
came across more deaders. The man carried a
briefcase and wouldn't let it out of his sight. More
than once he mumbled something about it being too
late. Inside the briefcase was the thumb drive, the
man's ID, and badge we found. The man was a
member of the bilateral forum between South Africa
and Britain. The thumb drive contained important
information that he was transporting to their
impromptu meeting in London. He didn't know the
nature of it, but understood it had something to do
with the zombies that kept crossing their paths.

He collected the goodies and stuffed everything
into his pockets when the dying man awoke as a
zombie. He lunged for him. Eshe got to his feet, but
not quickly enough. The man bit into his back, his

teeth cutting through the cloth of his shirt and sinking into his flesh. Eshe managed to shoot him, point blank, but the damage was already done. So it seemed the man was turning before he was bitten, further confirming my suspicions that bites didn't infect people with the zombie sickness.

I didn't get why the man with top secret information was flying a commercial airline but Eshe couldn't answer that question. I guessed the only reason the man told him so much was caused by delirium from the virus.

As we neared Jacksonville colorful clumps moved with the waves and the stench forced me to pull my shirt over my mouth and nose. I grabbed the binoculars and gasped at what I saw. Bodies, loads of bodies; hundreds, no thousands, washed up on shore with the tide. They moved back out with it. Never moving further than the coastline.

Destruction laid waste to the beach. Large homes, once glorious, now missing rooms and roofs, and the beach had shrunk. Trees intermingled with the bodies as they scooted on and off shore. It took my mind several minutes to process what I was seeing. When it clicked, it clicked. A hurricane hit the city. Jacksonville was the one place in Florida where it was relatively safe to own a beach house because the Gulf Stream was just off shore and moved large storms away from the city. Somehow, in the demise of the city's occupants, a monster of a storm swirled in the Atlantic or came up through the gulf and devastated the city. It barely looked like my home.

"What do you see?" asked Sarah. The gentle breeze blew her curls away from her face, displaying her inquisitive eyes.

"Bodies, lots of them." I handed her the binoculars.

She gasped, much like I had. Then her mouth dropped and words tumbled out, "What do you think happened?"

"A hurricane."

She chuckled. "I thought those hit south Florida."

"What else would destroy homes, topple trees, and wash the bodies onto shore like that?" I asked, my tone short.

"Here? I can't believe it. This is wild. I'm glad we missed it." She dropped the binoculars from her eyes.

That was it, end of conversation and I got her meaning, all too well. We'd been through everything imaginable and I was glad the thing hit when we were at sea instead of after we arrived. The sun beat hard against my head and sweat bubbled on my brow.

I informed the adults of what I'd spotted as a warning. We'd have to maneuver carefully through the waterlogged deaders and debris to make it back to the marina.

"It might be better to keep the boat offshore and send a small group onshore," offered my father.

The other adults nodded their heads in agreement and Heather spoke up, "I need to go and I need Maddie to come with me."

My mother involuntarily shuddered. Not quite a shudder, but more a body tick. She didn't like the idea but they'd said it; Bryce, Sarah, and I were adults in the new zombie world and we'd earned it. Mazi and Mesi had shown extreme skill and bravery too. She didn't say a word.

My father and Katrina agreed that I would be the best choice to go onshore with Heather. It was imperative, really, that I did. We'd learned so much together and needed to finish it together. Our ride from Cape Town, I'd been her assistant as we set up the office as a lab and tested blood samples, read notes, made more notes, and learned what made us immune. Or what we thought. We didn't have the fanciest equipment; only what we were able to take in the rush we were in from the deader torture lab in Cape Town. But our hypothesis was that it was a virus and what made us immune was genetic.

The virus bounced off my blood but with my mom, Heather, Katrina, Mazi, and Mesi it attached, made more viruses, but they soon died as their blood made antibodies to fight it. My father, Sarah, and Eshe, it had a different response. When it entered, the body immediately destroyed it. They already had antibodies, most likely from their fight with the disease. Heather said their bodies produced a protein -- the antibodies -- in response to the virus giving the body specific immunity. I had a natural immunity that I didn't completely understand. I vaguely remembered immunity from a biology lesson. She wanted to test living deaders, but good luck finding and catching some.

Our thinking was since my dad had been ill, and Sarah and Eshe bitten, their bodies built an immunity like a vaccine. Everyone else had some type of natural resistance and I was completely immune. *But why was I immune? What was different about me?* That's where she needed better equipment to test her hypothesis. She, no we, assumed it was my allergy to mosquitoes. Yeah, the one thing that would bloat me like a watermelon, and if untreated put me into anaphylactic shock, is the one thing that kept me from turning deader. Go figure!

Mazi volunteered to join us, but I suggested he stay. There needed to be people to complete food runs. He was handy with the scary double-sided ax and reluctantly agreed. My father maneuvered the yacht just outside the clearest deader area. They were still floating among the fallen trees and with gobs of algae stuck in between, but it looked like we had a narrow clear path. Heather and I slipped doctor masks over our faces to knock out the stench. Breathing my own air was far better than death, but still not my first choice.

I dared not look at their misshapen, sun burned faces. The bodies were beyond disgusting and I didn't want to see anyone I'd known. We managed to paddle as a team but it took several minutes to get the hang of it. At various points I used my paddle to push bodies out of the way but it did little good as another would pop up from below and take their spot. A cringe was painted on Heather's beautiful face, turning her lips upside down. This wasn't the nastiest thing I'd done but was at least an 8 on a 1 - 10 scale.

The shoreline ahead beckoned us. Its sandy beach beyond the rows of deaders was inviting if I didn't shift my eyes three feet forward.

"They're thickening. I don't think the boat's going to make it through," Heather stated, her voice testy. This wasn't something she wanted to do but something we had to do in order to find a cure or at least a vaccine. Something to protect the actual living from the next lovebug invasion. They came out twice yearly and the next would be soon; as in another month or so.

I twisted my brain to remember anything I'd learned about the St. Johns River. It was our major waterway in Florida and emptied into the ocean in Jacksonville somewhere. It was also one of the few rivers that flowed South to North which meant if we found by chance the mouth of it we'd be paddling against the flow. Luckily it wasn't a ferocious river and we didn't have any mountains to push us toward waterfalls.

Mentally, I located where we were, although I wasn't sure since everything looked so different. I pulled the compass out of my shirt. We were heading straight west. I sighed. "Let's move this thing north, maybe we'll find the mouth of the St. Johns. I don't know if it'll be better though."

"It's worth a try. The bodies are piled several deep and negotiating them is becoming a chore."

I agreed, but what was waiting for us in the river? The little life boat bumped and jumped over

deaders as we steered it due north, searching for the
the mouth of the St. Johns, and at one point my
paddle got stuck inside the hollowed body of a
deader. That made my mind scowl. *Where did its
insides go?*

It didn't take long for that question to be
answered. As we veered through the murky waters
of the St. Johns, a golden fin crested the water. My
body froze and my breath caught.

"What is that, Maddie?" Heather asked with a
quiet, shaky voice.

"Exactly what you think." I wasn't yet so sure,
but when a body pushed against its side and its jaw
opened wide we both knew what it was. A shark; a
golden yellow shark. Better know as a lemon shark.
In Jacksonville, if you didn't hunt and fish you did
one or the other, and I'd heard about them but never
heard of them eating people. In contrast, the sharks
here weren't considered a threat. I guessed this shark
didn't get the memo and I was sure living people
would be more of a delicacy than the dead ones.

She placed her paddle on her lap and whispered,
"What do we do?"

I was no shark expert. I had no clue, but we
didn't want his attention and not in our little blow-
up life boat. No doubt shark teeth could rip right
through the thick plastic. I absorbed our
surroundings and the bodies grew less dense further
inland, most likely because the river flowed north
and we were heading south. The banks of the
shoreline appeared mostly clear and a marina wasn't
far. "Maybe we can get to the shore?"

"Then what? We walk? How swampy is this area?" Heather asked with narrowed eyes.

I didn't know. Unlike the rest of the people in Jacksonville I didn't hunt or fish. "OK, if we don't move we'll go back out to the ocean."

She considered my words. We stared at each other for several seconds as one of us tried to come up with a plan. Another shark appeared, followed by another. Our odds were growing worse by the second. We needed to do something.

A chorus of screeching cut through the air. It sounded like a bunch of wild boars and forced us to cover our ears and duck. Vultures swooped down on the bodies, flapping and hissing at the sharks. "Now, we paddle away," I said firmly. Vultures were scavengers and enjoyed a good dead meal. As they fought over and distracted the sharks we had an out.

Heather wasted no time in dipping her paddle back into the water. We vigorously expended our energy moving down stream or up stream. I wasn't sure of the terminology. Anyway, it didn't matter, we were moving inland and away from wild nature.

Chapter Twenty-Three

I didn't look back as we paddled to the closest marina. Nothing would touch the deaders but sharks and vultures. Even the lion in Africa wouldn't go near them. It was easier going as the deaders all flowed out to the ocean. I guessed the storm that washed them into the water also washed them into the Atlantic. Jacksonville was a series a waterways; most commonly called the Intracoastal. Bridges spanned the city. The hurricane must have dumped a large amount of water which pushed the deaders out instead of gobbing up the mouth into the ocean like a dam.

We pulled the life boat to the closest marina and docked it. It wasn't the marina we left out of, but that didn't matter. If we were lucky we'd find a car or something we could use. No bodies lay on the ramp or in the parking lot. Nowhere. They were all washed up on the beach. We tried every car we found but no keys and neither of us knew Bryce's secret to hot wiring cars. My arms and body tired from paddling, I dropped onto a cement bench.

Heather dropped beside me. "We take a five minute break then we go. There's no time to waste and I don't want to be wandering this city in the dark. It creeps me out."

The last several weeks creeped me out, but I was beyond being scared anymore. It had become my life. Prickles still traced my spine and uneasy feelings settled in my belly but it was life. I pushed forward.

After our five minutes of rest, we stood and left the marina in search of wheels.

We found a van outside a hotel. It was the type they used to shuttle people from the airport. The keys were in it and a couple deaders. Reluctantly, we got to work, grimaces on our faces, and dragged the bodies out of the van.

They were pretty jellied by this point so we didn't really so much drag as we did fling them out of the van using our weapons and their luggage to scoot them towards the door. It was a messy job and Heather gagged several times. I really thought she was going to lose her breakfast but it must have been already digested because it didn't come back up.

I drove since I knew the city and how to find Bryce's house. We needed to find his dad -- dead or alive. Preferably alive, but I was prepared for dead. I didn't know how I'd break that news to Katrina or Bryce but I think maybe they accepted he may not be alive since Bryce last saw him turning deader.

The hot afternoon sun pounded our heads as we stepped out of the van at Bryce's house. Visions of Bryce the day we found each other coasted through my brain, followed by the preparations we took for the inevitable zombie apocalypse. We hadn't heard a word from him and Jack. Each day that went by, another knot twisted in my stomach that I'd never see him again. The cold metal of the compass bobbed against my chest as Heather pushed open the unlocked door. That was the thing about the military: they didn't bother to lock up after storming homes, businesses, hotels. They tossed the bodies into semi-orderly heaps and left.

Sunlight mingled with dust drifted through the living room, casting an eerie glow. The house was an open floor plan. The kitchen straight ahead, with a couple barstools against the flat granite counter top. The stainless steel appliances were nearly blinding as the sun's rays hit against them.

I turned my ear to listen but heard nothing. No hum of the refrigerator or clunks dropped from the ice maker. Not a single sound except our footsteps over the tile floor, and they were barely audible. There were open doorways on either side of the living room. Heather went in one direction and I went the other.

I rounded the corner to three partially open doorways. The first room was an office. Papers were strewn messily across the desk top. A sun-bleached area, almost perfectly square, was vacant of its usual occupant. Running my finger around the edges of the square, I drew a line in the settled dust. Four levels of wooden shelves held books and binders sitting in a precarious haphazard state. *Was Bryce's father always this messy?*

The way Bryce talked about him, I figured him for a mix of eccentric and OCD. The sun-bleached area of the desk caught the corner. From the angle I was standing the desk dust appeared thicker around the square than in the square. I returned and inspected further. It was thicker, much thicker, as if someone had taken the object. Judging by its shape, I assumed a lap top.

Turning on my heel, I stared again at the book shelves then ran into the next room. Thrusting the door open I stared at what I assumed was Bryce's room. His clothes still lay in a pile over the carpet, his bed unmade. The comforter sagged off one side while the sheets were bunched towards the back.

A hand touched my shoulder and I did a leap-spin move, lifting my ax high into the air.

"It's just me!" Heather said.

"Don't sneak up on a girl," I said, dropping the ax.

"He's not here. I'm not sure what that means," she said in exasperation.

On the yacht, Heather had read over the journals we brought and studied the black zombie heart I found. All they were doing in that facility was testing the dead. They tortured them, and I really felt bad. True, they were gross and I'd killed a few dozen or so, but those were compassion killings. *Who would really want to live with no quality of life and no hope to get it back?* Since Bryce's father was an environmental scientist we hoped to find more about how it started and how we could stop it. WEAC was ground zero and that's why we were now in Bryce's home searching for something that would tell us where the WEAC facility was.

I stepped out of the room and into the office. "I think he left on his own. In the dust is the imprint of a square object the size of a laptop."

She sighed. "I think you're right. Follow me."

A chair lay on its side in the hall. Heather pointed into the room. It was dark, as the curtains were pulled shut, but there was enough light to see the shambles of the room. Bedsheets were strewn across the floor; a broken lamp lay next to the bed, shattered in several large pieces. The dressers were barren on top as every item had been pushed to the floor as if in anger or... I didn't want to think about 'or'.

"I fancy this is the room Bryce locked him in, but he's not here now," Heather said in her proper accent.

I scratched my head. This had to be the room. I remembered Bryce saying he'd pushed a chair against it to keep him in. *Was he in one of the piles on the streets?*

Heather walked around me and closed the bedroom door. "You see this?"

Scratches -- all across the door. "We need light," I said as I coasted toward the window and pushed the curtain wide open. The scratches were long and jagged, as if done by claws.

"He was trying to get out." Heather's voice shook as she ran her finger gently across the grooves.

Heather pointed towards the door lock. "No, he did get out. See here? He took a knife and popped the door lock."

Bryce hadn't mentioned a door lock. "Maybe it was the military."

"I don't think so. It wouldn't be on the inside. It'd be on the outside then." She had a point, a very good one. He'd escaped with the dexterity of a living living person not a deader.

"He's alive!" I shouted.

"Yes, very much so. We need clues where he went. We need to know where the WEAC facility is located," Heather said, a hand on her hip.

"WEAC. It stands for... Wetland," I racked my brain. If only I could use my phone to keep notes. "Umm, Environment something Conservation."

"I have an idea." She checked the kitchen drawers, pulling each one out and set a thin, floppy book on the counter. Opening it, she sifted through the pages, using her finger to guide. "Here it is."

I glanced at the spot above her finger. *You've got to be kidding me. It was in the yellow pages, holy fizz pops!* That was it. That's where he was. I ran through the kitchen and threw open the garage door. The eerie darkness settled on me. The corners could hide any type of creature. A single small car was parked in the middle. I slammed the door and locked it. Shivers ran over my spine.

The car had to be his mom's but where was Bryce's? He'd taken his dad's van the day we all boarded Earnest Earl to parts filled with zombies, volcanoes, and tsunamis. I scurried back to Heather who was now waiting with an expectant face by the front door.

"He took Bryce's car!" I shot.

We headed back into the bright sunlight and loaded into the van we sort of borrowed or stole. I still didn't really know which, and was positive it didn't matter. A pit stop at a local gas station provided us with a map. I kept my head high to avoid the faces of the dead and clutched my ax.

Chapter Twenty-Four

Without GPS it was tough finding WEAC even with the map we took with the tank of gas. The road took us far into Jacksonville swamp land and dead ended. An airboat was conveniently located on the grass but it was tilted on its side like everything else. Whatever ravaged the city took no pity and had no prejudices. Using the van, we tipped the airboat then, once on its bottom, we climbed onboard.

Everything was working great -- even the keys were in the ignition! One slight problem; neither of us had any clue how to drive it. It didn't have a wheel like most boats. A big lever, it did have.

Heather turned the key. After a few sputters it started right up. She lowered her brows. "Now what?"

"Wiggle the big lever," I suggested. *What else could it be?*

She wiggled it and it jerked forward then stopped. I glanced at her. She was focused on the stick, and then pulled it back and we lurched off the grass into the water, full speed ahead.

"How do you slow this thing down?!" she yelled above the rattling motor.

"Push it the other direction."

She did and it stalled.

"Maybe you should take this. You have more of a way with boats," she proposed, wide eyed.

Great! Great! I repeated in my mind. The British lady was scared of an airboat. I gave her the benefit of the doubt as we exchanged seats. Maybe, possibly, they didn't have swamp areas in the UK for such vehicles.

I turned the key again. It sputtered and caught then I gently pulled the lever backwards. The boat glided over the water slowly. I moved the stick to the left and the right attempting to determine the steering without going full throttle. After a few minutes I started to get the hang of it but cruised along slow.

"At this rate we will get there in the A.M."

I snapped back, "But at least we'll get there in one piece without a swim in the stinky, murky water." The good news was no dead deaders were anywhere to be seen. We really didn't have much clue where we were going. The map was useless at this point, so I learned as we rode. At first I took corners too sharp and scraped the grassy land area more than once. We bounced over a patch or two of slim, grassy land strips. The sun took leave and I hadn't a clue where the lights on the thing were, so we cruised in the darkness.

"Look," she pointed, "ahead. There are lights."

I peered through the inky, foggy darkness and about a football field away were dim lights. That meant one of two things; either we found WEAC, or someone was out there. I was hoping more for WEAC than a human.

I kept the boat steady. As we drew closer, the outline of a large rectangular building took shape.

Adrenaline pulsed through my veins. *Was this it? Did we find it?*

I drove the boat up the grassy patch of land until it rested within a foot or so of the building. That was more accidental, as I wasn't sure where the brakes were or how to stop the thing. I was simply hoping we didn't crash into the building. The lights were much brighter now through the haze. Clearly there were no deaders and obviously it had electricity, probably from an industrial-size generator.

We scrambled out of the boat and a male voice caught our attention. I jumped at his words.

"Stop, both of you," his voice soft but firm. It was followed by the distinct shink shink of a shot gun.

I didn't turn around and was surprised at how tiny the sound of my words were as they tumbled out of my mouth. The man resembled heavily the man in the pictures at Bryce's home. "Are you... Mr. uhhh... Bryce's father?" I couldn't remember his name. *Did Bryce ever tell me?*

"Who are you?" he asked. His words shook at the end as if he was nervous. The last nervous guy with a gun ended up sick from a zombie bite. *That ended OK, but would this?*

"I'm Heather. That is Maddie. If you are Bryce's father, you are the man we are looking for." Heather's voice was fluid and fantastically British. Not a hint of fear, but more of excitement.

"Where is Bryce?" he asked, his voice no longer shaky but solid and firm like a cement floor.

I turned and stared at a man, fortyish, hair surrounding the bald gap on top that sparkled in the light. A pocket protector with a couple pens on his light colored shirt. He was good looking despite the bald patch. I wondered if it was hereditary. I loved Bryce's long hair. *Would he one day lose it?* I shook the thought and answered his question. "He's not here. If you let us in we'll tell you everything."

He wiggled his thin brows and dropped the shotgun to his side. "How can I trust you?"

Lowering the shotgun showed me he already trusted us, or was willing to give us the benefit of the doubt. *How long had he been here? How did he escape the house and why hadn't he turned?* The questions rolled through my head like a freight train.

Heather elbowed my side and whispered, "The compass, Maddie."

A fabulous idea! My mind wanted the answers, but in order to get them we needed something; something that showed we in fact knew Bryce. I dug it out from beneath my shirt. The gold coating caught the moonlight. I strolled closer to him as I pulled it over my head. I held it out in front of him.

He lifted it off my hand and turned it over, his eyes still fixed on the golden object, he said, "Leland Price. Follow me." He wrapped his fingers around the compass and didn't give it back right away.

The WEAC facility was located deep into the Intracoastal on a patch of land not much larger than the building. He opened the door and white light flooded us, causing me to squint my eyes. As they adjusted I took in the white walls, ceiling, and floor that made the place bright enough I had to squint again as my eyes adjusted to the influx of light and gave it a sterile appearance.

The undeniable odor of bleach blasted my nostrils, covering the smell I would never forget -- death. People had died here, probably turned zombie. How many had he killed to take over the facility? Surely it wasn't empty when he arrived. We followed him into a room that was far easier on the eyes. The walls were a light tan, the floor carpeted, and a small, unmade twin bed was in the corner. Four brown fabric chairs sat around a square table and to the left was a kitchenette and next to that a simple metal computer desk with a laptop. There were four other doors. I imagined one was a restroom. It was cozy, kind of. Obviously where he'd been living.

I got on with our story, starting with how Bryce and I met. He blinked his eyes rapidly and asked, "You and Bryce shared a dream?"

Duh, that's what I said. "We did," I concurred.

He stood, placed a finger over his lips. "That's not possible," he mumbled and began pacing.

"It is and it happened." The news had visibly shaken him. It was strange, but no stranger than the majority of people in the world dying of a mysterious virus.

He shook his head and halted. "Are you sure?"

I was getting a bit over it and snapped, "That's what I said, isn't it?"

"It's impossible for two people to share a dream, interact, and bring an object out of it, unless it was engineered."

It never made sense to me either, but it happened, and so did too many other things that were even weirder, so I hadn't given it much thought.

Heather interjected, "Engineered, how?"

He stumbled over his words, "I... I... don't," he paused for a second, "know. The government maybe. They knew this was coming."

I cleared my throat. "How do you know that? Did you know?"

He shook his head. "No. I knew something big was happening but not what. I had suspicions that some type of secret testing was happening here but never found anything. It was a gut feeling."

"Were there specific actions that gave you this 'gut feeling'? Heather inquired.

He lowered his eyes and raked a hand over his balding head. "This is one of the facilities I monitor and their actions were suspicious. They said they were studying sustainable mosquito control, which means gene splicing in today's scientific world. During my visits there were parts of the facility I never saw and on one occasion they appeared to be loading materials into an airboat. When I asked, they changed the subject. I reported this to my superiors who didn't seem at all concerned. I found the research and there's more but, please, I want to know about my family."

My questions had questions, and I'm sure Heather's did too, but giving him peace of mind was the priority so I told him our story from the beginning.

"So my family is alive?"

Heather and I nodded.

"And Bryce, he's still alive too?"

That I couldn't guarantee, but since we had some type of extra special connection I didn't feel that he was anything but alive. "I think so."

Water coated my eyes and my nose twitched from the strength of the bleach. It bothered me, not just physically. It was the smell of death underneath. It was stronger in this room and smelled as though it was moving through the walls.

"It's your turn," stated Heather, all business. She wanted the answers. The purpose of our visit was the technology the facility was likely to have. What she had on the boat was limited. She didn't simply want a vaccine, but a way to stop the virus in the future. The virus could mutate in the next batch of bugs and kill every last human.

"I'm sorry. I've been very rude. Would you like water or a snack?" he offered, completely avoiding her question as he padded to the refrigerator and opened the door.

I was hungry, thirsty, and tired, but also curious. He grabbed two waters and placed them on the table. I didn't waste time in chugging mine. Heather was more reserved as she took it off the table, unscrewed the cap, and took a swig.

The wheels in Heather's head were turning. I saw it in her expression and posture. She wanted to grill him, here and now. Her chest filled with air as she took a deep breath and let it out. The warmth of it moved past my nose, dissipating the bleach-death odor for a second.

He took a seat. "I was turning, or I thought I was. I tried to warn Bryce. There isn't much I remember. The days were clouded with images. My family; people staring at me from outside, pawing at the window to get in. When my mind cleared I had splinters embedded in my fingers and under my nails. He dropped his hands onto the table, palms up, and with his thumb smoothed over the scars on his fingers.

He didn't glance up but kept his eyes lowered. "It was a dream and the only thing I remembered was telling Bryce to come here. All the answers are here. With that in mind, I escaped my house with no idea how I'd been locked in that room until today. I know he did it for the good of the people. If I'd turned I'd have only infected more. It was the fact that I didn't turn and the experiments. The environmental disaster that started here, inside these walls. I had to make it right." He nervously wiggled his mouth and chewed intermittently between words on his upper lip. In a quick motion he pushed back his chair and stood.

"You saw them loading an airboat as if they were moving something. Do you have any idea where they went?" Heather tilted her head his way in full expectation of an answer.

A scratching caught my eardrum and I twisted to find it. Maybe it was my imagination. His story spooked me and after everything I'd been through the last thing I wanted to admit to anyone, including myself, was that I was completely freaked out, more so than I had been. The place made me uneasy and knowing now that I was really inside ground zero gave my blood a rush.

"I found a note and journals filled with data. They accidentally found a way to control the mosquito population. A virus. It was planted in decaying material where the lovebug larva ate it as they grew. It did no harm until they laid more eggs and reached the end of their lifecycle, then they self-destructed. Their acids spraying over a small area. It effectively destroyed the mosquito larva population, reducing the number of adult mosquitoes, but was still under testing. Essentially the virus itself moves into every cell of the lovebug, turning it into a mush that explodes." He let out a breath and traced his finger in a small circle over the table top.

The scratching came again. Heather and Mr. Price, Bryce's Father, continued their discussion. *Was it all in my head?* My heart pounded hard inside my chest, knocking to free itself. *Calm down, Maddie,* I whispered inside my head. The katana I picked up in Cape Town was strapped to my back.

"Do you have a restroom?" I asked. It wasn't only that the water had washed right through me. The sound was growing louder. Scratching, as if someone was trying to free themselves. A clink followed the scratching.

Instead of pointing me to one of the four doors, he pointed me in the direction of the hall. Back in the blinding white hall, I shut the door and did my business. The scratching grew louder as I exited the bathroom. I pulled the katana from my back and stalked further down the hall, following the sound. The smell of death much more distinct the further into the facility I went. The bleach did little to cover it over. *Did he trap them all inside this place? Was it some type of fail safe? Or had they found us, smelled us out and gotten inside?*

I halted in my tracks when a low moan filled my ears. Death was here!

Chapter Twenty-Five

The sound was loud and close. It was on the other side of the wall but the door required a badge that I didn't have. I pressed my ear against the wall, listening intently. Low growling and scratches vibrated through the wall.

"What are you doing?"

I abruptly turned on my heel. "There's something on the other side of the wall!"

Mr. Price nodded. "Yes, I was just telling Heather about Dr. Stressal. She was the lead scientist. When I got to the facility she was the only one here and was locked inside this room. I've left her there." He slid a card over the slot and we followed him through another blinding white room. Glass separated us from zombie Dr. Stressal.

A live zombie! "Why didn't you kill her?"

He shrugged. "I couldn't, and maybe her body had answers. Her notes have certainly been helpful."

I looked at him expectantly, waiting. After several seconds he began, "Besides the development of the virus, I found a letter she wrote. The testing here was leaked to South Africa. Soon followed by China and Japan. Within several months every developed country and continent with mosquito problems were negotiating the new discovery. She claimed it was false and moved all the research and testing to an unknown location with only a skeleton crew working on it. The government found nothing."

He continued, "The problem was the new genetically altered lovebugs were born with the virus which meshed with the insects' DNA making a new breed that are stronger, faster, and larger. They were a success as mosquito populations declined at first. It wasn't until the first human was infected that they realized how dangerous the virus was. Essentially it does the same thing inside a human, moving from one cell to the next, the body quickly moving through stages of rigor mortis until eventually it will explode if not destroyed ahead of time. It's airborne, but stays viable in water for an unknown amount of time and can be transported that way and by amphibians."

Amphibians. I thought back to frog dissection and the yellowish mottled eggs. *Were they infected? They were dead, right?* The poor frogs were carriers. Since I didn't think the school would purchase infected frogs on purpose it made my mind spin. "What happens to a virus when its host dies?"

Heather looked at me blankly. "The virus dies."

"So why didn't the military destroy the bodies? Burn them or something?"

They both stared at me quizzically. This whole thing was an environmental nightmare of epic proportions, but wouldn't it make sense to dispose of the bodies?

Mr. Price spoke up, "The virus is airborne. True, a virus dies when its host dies, but since this lives in water it's possible any form of disposing of them might spread the virus."

That gave me a lot to think about. I didn't want to spend my life staring at decaying deaders.

He paused for a moment. "I think the government knows about this place. I heard the military come through and fly over it with their helicopters but no one came close. I believe Dr. Stressal was in touch with someone on the outside. This place runs on solar and is fully functional, including Wi-Fi."

Curiouser and curiouser. They were counting on her to stop this thing but had to know she was dead. In her condition, she hadn't responded to them in some time.

Two weeks later...

Dr. Stressal's blank eyes stared towards and around me. She chittered as she bit at the gag wrapped tightly around her mouth. The latex of the gloves did little to mask the coldness of her arm as I held it in place.

Bryce's father found her here, alone, going through the motions as if the virus hadn't taken over her body. We now knew that the zombies weren't truly dead. They had heartbeats, slow but present. They breathed. They smelled and heard noises. Their bodies were past the point of recovery and their brain functions limited, but they were still alive. My amateur suspicions had been correct since they had little more action in their heads than the function of the brain stem.

The fresh blood samples Heather had gotten from Dr. Stressal was what she needed for her final tests and the makings of a vaccine. Blood samples

and tests run on her blood showed it was too late for
Dr. Stressal. Combining any sample of our blood
with hers didn't have an effect on hers. At first it
appeared to, but that was simply our antibodies at
work. Her blood remained infected. *Could our blood
serve as a vaccine to those still alive? Or were those people
already like us?* The people carted away by the
military, and those in places far enough hidden the
military hadn't found them.

Heather inserted the needle into Dr. Stressal's
arm and pulled another vial of blood. Partially
coagulated chunks of red blotted the creamy
yellowish plasma.

Bryce's father continued Dr. Stressal's work. At
first her notes made sense but as the virus hit here
harder they made less sense until they were scribbles.
Her notes were detailed, as if she hoped someone
would come along and finish the job.

It was almost as if it was a confession; as if she
and she alone were responsible for the mess. She
hadn't done it alone but with a team. It did,
however, answer a lot of questions.

Aside from that, the virus no longer affected
mosquito larvae as they'd evolved. At first it killed
most but those few grew a resistance to the virus
making it no longer effective. The good news was
the mosquitoes didn't carry the virus like those of us
alive. They were immune. I had something in
common with the creepy bugs that blew me up like a
watermelon.

Bryce's father was working on genetically
altering the virus so it would kill the lovebugs before

hatching. It wouldn't be long before the fall lovebug season. He was working fast with few breaks, which included the days we brought him to the boat and his wife and daughter.

"Maddie," sounded my mother's voice from the radio placed on the counter only feet from me. Heather nodded her head for me to get it as she pulled the needle from the doctor's arm.

"I'm here, Mom."

"There's a military ship. It's still a ways out but appears to be headed to Jacksonville." Her voice didn't hide her fear.

And I didn't hide mine. "Where are you?"

"We're safe. We docked in a crowded port. The yacht blends with the others and the deaders here are dead."

A bit relieved, but what was the ship coming here for? The military had already been here. The evidence was everywhere.

Living with scientists who worked day and night, I took up preparing meals. They had to eat. My mind wandered and obsessed on how to dispose of the dead. I dropped three slices of spam into the frying pan then skimmed through the cabinet for a vegetable.

"Maddie." Heather burst into the kitchen. "I figured it out." Breathless from the excitement, she took a moment to catch her breath. "I tested it with mosquito saliva. That's what makes a person allergic. The proteins in their saliva. You have antigens like A and B but not the same. Yours are different. They make you highly allergic to mosquitoes but act like a shield to the virus. When the virus touches them a shield-like structure surrounds your cells. Your blood is a new blood type. That's not uncommon. History has shown that, during an epidemic, organisms evolve."

Great! It was now confirmed scientifically that I was a freak! A walking genetic mutation. I was speechless.

A glint of expectation lit up her eyes as she waited for me to speak, but what was there to say? She continued, "Maddie, I don't think you're alone. An epidemic on a scale this large, there has to be more people like you."

I flipped the spam in the pan. Now I felt better. There were a few other freaks out there too. "What does this mean? How does it help us?"

"I don't know yet. I've made a possible vaccine but have nothing to test it on, but your blood is special. You're the future of the human race!"

My brain was on overload and about to be further overloaded. I finished up the spam and collected Mr. Price. He and Heather talked over dinner. They talked in a language I couldn't understand. It was too smart-person-scientific for me but I caught the drift. My antigens were possibly the key to controlling the virus and eliminating the environmental threat. It included more splicing and my blood.

Chapter Twenty-Six

Bryce

He lay, not uncomfortably, on the mattress of the small twin bed. They'd trapped him in the room after sending Jack on a mission. Bryce had asked to go but they refused and put him in the room instead. The light blue walls gave him a sense of unease but the foreboding in his gut came from the locked door. When he arrived at the base they took a sample of his blood and let him go shortly after. He wasn't given free reign of the base but wasn't in the solitary confinement as he was now.

The door creaked open. A person in a hazmat suit walked in. He wasn't sick. Bryce rose onto his elbows. "What's going on?" he demanded.

Judging by the size and build he assumed it was a woman, although the bulky awkward suit made it hard to tell. "Sit up and hold out your arm please."

"Not until you tell me why I'm here. You can't lock me in here. I was promised I could come and go. I want to see the commander."

"The commander ordered this for your protection."

That made no sense at all. "I won't give you anything until I speak with him." Bryce folded his arms over his chest.

"He's not cooperating," she said to her suit after pushing a small button.

A large man in a hazmat walked through the door and forced Bryce's arms to the bed. Bryce wiggled his body, attempting to free himself, and pushed the man's chest with his feet but he was like an iron weight and Bryce's fight was futile.

A sharp pain like a needle struck Bryce in the neck and his vision immediately faded and his struggle ceased.

When he awoke hours later he was alone in the room and laid spread-eagled on the bed. He attempted to bring his arms to his sides but they wouldn't budge. His wrists twisted in the straps. His ankles too. *What was happening?*

It was a ruse. The whole thing. He shouldn't have trusted the military, and what about Jack? *Was he safe?* He'd watched him board the ship and seen it leave the port. A sinking feeling hit his gut. *Jack was in on it!* He was ex Coast Guard and had been so determined to find out what the military was up to. The purpose was to trap him, test him, and what about his family? They weren't safe! Bryce squeezed his eyes. *Why hadn't he figured this out sooner?*

He had to get free. The straps were leather and they didn't feel too tight. He wiggled and pulled, trying to free his hands. Voices in the hall stopped outside his door. He couldn't make out the words but the tone was low like a male's. He wiggled his hands further but couldn't get the straps past the fat part of his hand but was convinced he could if he worked it for a while -- leather stretched.

The voices continued as mumbles on the other side of the door. He scanned the ceiling and walls for a vent, a window, some way out of the room. The voices became quiet and footfalls moved away from the room then the door creaked.

Chapter Twenty-Seven

Maddie

"Maddie, come in," sounded through the static of the radio. I took it everywhere with me, including the shower. I stepped away from the shower head, leaving shampoo on half my head and leaned over, patting my hands dry, then clicked the radio.

"Sarah."

"Maddie, they found us and boarded the yacht. We just went for a food run and now we can't get back."

A sharp pain stung my heart. My family, Bryce's family, they were on the yacht. "What do you mean and who are 'they'?"

"The military and I think one of them is Jack. I'm sure one of them is…" Squawk! Static filled the distance between us.

"Where are you, Sarah?"

More static. "Sarah, come in. Where are you?"

"Where we were the moment it all began." The words came out loud and clear then more static.

"Sarah?" The only response was dead airwaves. I had to go. The marina. She was at the marina where my father docked Earnest Earl.

I rinsed the rest of the shampoo from my head and stepped out of the shower. I quickly dressed in jeans, sneakers, and a T-shirt then grabbed my katana and slid it into the strap on my back then clipped the radio to my pants and dropped the compass over my neck so it nestled snugly against my chest. I never went anywhere without my useless phone either. I pushed the door open and caught Mr. Price in the hall.

"Where are you going?" he asked, his brows flat.

I swallowed. "The military found the yacht. My family and yours are on it. I have to go now."

He put a hand out as if to stop me. "You think the military is going to hurt them?"

I didn't have time for this and pushed past him. "Yes, I think it's a possibility."

Heather heard the commotion and joined me at the door. "I'm joining you Maddie. You can't do this alone."

I let out a frustrated breath. "The work you're doing here is important and there's no one else to do it – besides, I'm not alone. Sarah is waiting for me." It turned out my blood was really quite useless but a vaccine could be made from those with antibodies.

Before either of them could get another protest in I pushed through the door. I'd gotten used to steering the airboat as I used it for food and supply runs. It was really a piece of cake. I coasted it onto the grass, cut it off and climbed into the airport shuttle.

Lightning streaked the sky, followed by rumbles of thunder. The normal late afternoon Jacksonville thunderstorm was quickly approaching. I ignored it as my mind was preoccupied with pulling off a rescue. I didn't know what we'd do when I got to them or if they already had a plan. My heart pumped hard inside my chest as my mind went through the motions of sneaking onto the yacht. I knew every inch of it. A more horrifying thought struck me, what if they'd transported them to the military carrier? *And was Jack really involved?* I'd come to trust him. That might have been a mistake; or maybe the military were the good guys.

It was possible? No, Dr. Stressal had been in contact with someone. They'd left WEAC alone, flew right over it. That could only mean one thing in my mind. They had orders not to touch it and the military was behind this.

The shuttle sputtered and coasted to a stop, breaking up my thoughts. Crap! I hadn't checked the gas and the pointed red line was on E. I'd learned it was best practice to stay prepared which meant I had a filled gas can in the back along with a few other supplies like food, a flashlight, and blankets.

I clicked open the gas cap from the inside then went around the side and slid the door open then dragged the gas can closer where I could get a good grip on it. The can was full and heavy. The first rain drop hit my head and rolled down my cheek.

Hurriedly, I went to work and emptied the gas can into the tank. I'd have to fill it again before returning to WEAC. That was another kink in any plan I needed to work out. The rain came hard as I slid the can back into the van. The thunder and lightning only seconds apart meant it was close. Now drenched, I climbed inside and started the shuttle. It sputtered at first, as the gas ran through the engine, then caught.

Back on the road, I was only a few minutes from the marina. The rain poured over the windshield in buckets hindering my visibility and making me nervous. I wasn't an experienced driver and hadn't ever driven through a storm. A blast almost as loud as a grenade pierced my ears and fire encapsulated the shuttle. It lasted only seconds then smoke filled the cabin and it rolled to a stop.

My breath caught as my mind sorted through what happened. I'd been struck by lightning. I let out a breath. My only choice now was to walk it. I shone my flashlight through the window. I needed somewhere safer to wait this thing out. Off the bank of the freeway was a housing development on one side surrounded by a large barrier wall and an office complex through a light grouping of trees.

I chose the office complex. Securing the katana on my back and grabbing the flashlight, I jumped out of the vehicle and ran towards the trees. Mud splashed against my pants as my feet sank into the saturated ground. I dodged tree limbs until reaching the parking lot. It was empty of life, only a few stranded vehicles.

I shined the light across the length of the building. Once I located a door, I bolted across the parking lot and thrust it open.

Rain was the only sound as it pattered against the building. The beam from my flashlight lit up the hallway. What I saw made me grip the katana tighter.

Chapter Twenty-Eight

Two dead zombie eyes stared at me. I knew that was more a reflex. It couldn't see me. Its long gray hair hung limp on its shoulders as it clicked its tongue, blood dribbling from its mouth on its way towards me. Its drip drag stagger-walk was impressively quick. A flowered sundress covered in sprays of blood, chunks of human skin clung to the fabric.

On the floor behind her was a man in a black robe. His mouth was in an O as he screamed, "No!"

I swung the blade of the katana towards her dirty, slimy neck when she came within a few feet of me. It nearly connected then something I'd never seen, nor imagined, happened. The zombie blew apart from the inside out. I was glad my teeth were gritted as I'd have had a mouth full of deader if I hadn't. Chunks and blood sprayed the walls. It was a definite ten on my disgusting scale.

Chunks of her blew into the man's mouth. He gagged and spat to rid his body of the nasty zombie meal. His face met mine and he scooted backwards on the floor. His eyes barely visible through the zombie mess covering it. I moved closer to him. He was living. "Are you hurt?"

"You killed her!" he growled. "You are a murderer!"

What? I hadn't expected that one and I hadn't killed her; she blew up like one of Deavers' grenades.

"I didn't kill her. She was infected and there's no cure. Did she bite you?"

"You killed my wife." He continued sliding backwards.

That's when I noticed it. The beam from my flashlight caught the silver barrel of a gun, only a couple feet from him. I moved towards him. "Don't think about or you'll be dead like your wife."

He scooted again and I moved quicker now and jabbed the end of the katana's blade into his chest. Keeping it centered on him, I side-stepped and kicked the gun. It flew across the floor.

"Get up!" I ordered with a sneer.

He pushed his back against the wall and slid up it. His short, dark hair was coated in zombie film. I jabbed the blade lightly into his chest so he knew I meant business. When I did, it slid through a hole in the dark robe hanging around his shoulders. "Did she bite you, Professor?" I didn't know what else to call him and it looked similar to a graduate's robe.

His Adam's apple bobbed as he swallowed. "That makes no difference. Go. Go now!"

Well, this wasn't going well. The patter of rain stopped, meaning the worst of the storm was over. I glanced over the hallway. A collar of sorts clung to the wall in the muck. I grabbed it. "You've been keeping her alive, treating her like a pet?" That was sick. Really sick and morbid.

He narrowed his eyes into tiny slits. A chunk of deader flesh dropped from his forehead. "She was my wife."

The memory of my father turning seemed like a million years ago but it was still fresh in my head. I knew he was turning and that I should kill him, but I didn't. Instead we tied him up. This guy did the same thing. He put a collar around her neck. I brought the katana to my side. "I don't want to kill you and I didn't kill her. She exploded. I've never seen that before." Mr. Price's words rattled through my brain. The lovebugs were genetically engineered to explode. "When did she turn?"

"In the beginning. The very beginning."

That begged a lot of questions like *how did you get her past the military? What has she been eating? Was that why her drip-drag was so quick?*

The rain stopped and I was on a mission. "We have to go."

"I'm not going anywhere with you."

I rolled my eyes. I needed some answers and he would provide them. "Yes, you are. Remember I have the weapon and you don't. I also have your wife's collar and I bet it's a shock collar. The kind used for training dogs." I smirked.

"Fine," he seethed.

I lifted the katana towards his chest again and spread the cloth of his robe. What I saw didn't surprise me. A set of round, fresh, human-deader teeth marks. I lifted the collar towards him with my free hand. "Put this on just in case."

He didn't know I was completely immune and I wasn't entertaining him with that tidbit. The collar was more to keep him close. I wanted to know if someone bitten by a zombie who'd already feasted on human flesh turned.

Reluctantly he grabbed the collar and wrapped it around his neck. The motion caused a chunk of flesh to fall from his robe, revealing a name tag.

"You first, Alvah." I read the tag.

For the next hour we steadily walked towards the marina and I pried all sorts of information from him. He was a Duval County judge. That explained the black robe. He and his wife were visiting family in Gainesville when the end of the world went down. She was exposed immediately but didn't turn until a couple days later. Dumb luck saved them from the military. They'd spent the night in their RV deep in the woods. When he woke up the next morning his wife, Gloria, was eating their Pomeranian. I imagined large puffs of fur stuck between her teeth and chuckled.

"It's not funny!" he growled.

He was wrong. It was funny. In this new world I had to find humor where I could and that was hilarious. However, I stopped laughing out of respect and let him continue his story.

"I tied her up with bungee cords and glanced a peek out of the window. I would have waved my hands and let them take me, but they'd have killed Gloria. I couldn't have that. A soldier approached the RV, I stood inside with my gun loaded and waited. A radio voice came through, "Need help now! Surrounded by them." That was it. They never returned and I got us out of there."

"You may turn you know."

He nodded.

"I'll be forced to kill you when you do."

He nodded.

The truth was I didn't know if he'd turn but I was surely going to find out. The marina was ahead. I hadn't thought to bring binoculars but the coast looked clear at first glance. We ducked behind Mr. Price's van. The sun was just peeking over the horizon. "Do you see anything?"

The chain from the collar tugged. I glanced over my shoulder to see him convulsing. *Was this it?* No, after several seconds the seizure stopped. I pulled the handle to the back door of the van. Perfect: it wasn't locked. "Get in."

It was exactly as we left it, including the keys in the ignition. A wave of memories from that first day flooded me. I shook them out and focused on now. Gripping the radio I called, "Sarah, come in." There was no response. "Sarah." Again, no response. My stomach did flip flops. *Was I too late?*

I yanked his collar and stared him the eyes. "We need to find her." Through the nastiness coating him it was difficult to tell if he was losing his color but his awkward movements told me something was happening inside him.

I opened the van door. "You first."

With semi-mechanical movements he stepped out of the van and crumpled to the pavement, pulling me with him. I let go of the leash to avoid toppling onto him and quickly picked it back up once my feet hit the pavement.

"Maddie," sounded a whisper.

"Sarah," I whispered back.

A bob of hair and a set of eyes peered over the crate Bryce and I hid behind in the premonition. It wasn't Sarah's eyes nor hair but Mazi's. "Move," I ordered him.

Unsteadily, he lifted himself off the ground. We moved towards the crate and I lowered myself once we reached it. A gentle breeze from the water blew a chunk of matted hair fallen from my ponytail across my mouth. I blew it away.

"What is that?" Mazi asked, his eyes locked onto Alvah who stood, his arms propped against the top of the crate.

I leaned and whispered into Mazi's ear, "He was bit by his zombie wife who had already eaten living humans."

Mazi's eyebrows lowered and his face turned into a scowl. "Leave him here."

"No," I shook my head. "We might be able to use him and I want to know if he turns."

"That's sick, Maddie. Put him out of his misery."

The chain in my hand jerked. Alvah was glaring at us. "I can hear you and no one is putting me out of my misery. Is that clear?" His voice was concise.

Mazi nodded and flashed an icy glare my way. "Come on. They're inside the office. We figured you'd find us there."

Mesi and Sarah's eyes went wide when we entered the tiny building.

"What happened to you?" asked Mesi.

In the exact moment Mesi asked her question Sarah scowled, "Really, Maddie, a pet zombie?"

"I'm not a pet or a zombie! Not yet!" Alvah scowled.

I laughed out loud. The situation was entertaining. All eyes glared at me.

"You laugh at the most insane and insensitive moments," stammered Alvah

I laughed harder and accidentally pushed the button that sent an electric shock to the collar. Alvah jerked like a robot with a short circuit.

Soon Mazi, Mesi, and Sarah joined me in laughter that subsided after a few minutes.

Alvah glared at us, a frown evident on his face from the crusty lines encircling his mouth. At least the shock hadn't done any permanent damage. I blew out a breath. "The keys are still in the van, let's roll."

We traveled south, taking backroads. The drive gave us time to talk. The cabinets in the yacht were near bare. What was in them wouldn't feed them for the remainder of the day. They couldn't afford to wait out the carrier. Assuming they were far enough away from the ship, it was decided someone would go on a food run. The three of them volunteered. It was on their return they spotted action on the yacht and noted the military's presence. One man, Sarah swore was Jack.

They dropped the food and, on foot, made it to the marina. That's when they radioed me. At this point we didn't know if they were still on the yacht or if the military had forced them onto the carrier. What disappointed me most about all of it was Jack.

He'd proved himself to be a decent man but even decent men could change during hard times.

I parked the van outside Mayport Naval Station and we crept stealthily towards the base. There were no guards posted at the gates so it was easy to get onto the base. Now it got trickier, and we had to stay behind buildings and vehicles as we moved closer to the port.

Alvah seized again, jerking the chain between us. I stopped, kicking his convulsing body into the wall of a building. I didn't need him alerting them.

"Leave him," suggested Mesi.

I shook my head. "No, he's coming with us. I have a plan."

Alvah stopped convulsing. "Are you there?" I hit his cheek.

"Ouch," came a belated response.

He hadn't turned yet, but I didn't think it would be long. Drool fell from the side of his mouth, leaving a streak through the zombie grime of his dead wife.

I turned to the group and quickly inventoried their weapons. They all brandished the katanas we'd picked up in Cape Town except Mazi. He had the double-headed ax. No gun. "Get to the ship and save them. Alvah and I are going straight up the middle, into the open. Run, I'm your distraction. Radio Heather when you get somewhere safe. She will guide you to WEAC."

I knew this might be the end for me but I had to try it and we were no match for the military with their weapons and man power. I took a deep breath and pulled Alvah along.

"I'm turning... aren't you scared... I'll bite you?" Alvah's words came labored and breathless.

I ignored him but pulled him closer, using him as a human shield. We'd walked nearly half the distance of a football field when words came through a loudspeaker.

"Stop! Don't move any closer." The words were followed by the sound of footsteps from all sides. Within moments, soldiers came into view. Masks on their faces, M-16s in their hands -- aimed at us.

I pulled Alvah closer, so close his back was pressed against my side. Stepping in circles about twenty-five sets of eyes stared at me. *I was one girl with one semi-deader, did they really think I could hurt them?*

"Don't come closer," I shouted. "I'm alive. Him, not so much. I don't go anywhere without him. If you shoot him, you shoot me and I have something you need." I'd have to bargain and I'd probably be taken in against my will and separated from my zombie turning friend but I had to give it a try.

"Let him go, Maddie." Light glinted off the all too familiar head as Jack moved closer towards me. "We have to kill him but we don't want to kill you."

I couldn't believe it. Rage filled me up. "Where is my family, Jack?"

He continued his stroll towards me as if I posed no threat. Jack wasn't present when Heather took samples of blood, so I didn't know if he was immune and even if he was would that include a bite from an infected individual that already ate a human?

I knew aside from Alvah's bite he also probably ingested parts of his wife when she exploded. "Don't come closer."

Every minute stretched as I did my best to give Sarah, Mazi, and Mesi time to evacuate my family. The sun burned against the gunk covering my body, making me smell as bad as one of the deaders. I didn't think I'd get the smell out of my nose anytime soon.

Alvah groaned and holding him close to me was the equivalent of controlling a pit bull. He was changing, smelled them, wanted a bite. *I was closer, why not me?* Maybe it was the coating of death that covered me. From my peripheral vision I spotted a marine vessel cruise out from the below the ship. "Alvah," I whispered in his ear as I jerked his head towards my face.

He turned and for a moment his eyes met mine and a glint of recognition fluttered then they went dead and his mouth opened wide. "That's it, bite me." I was taking a chance but if what Heather discovered about my blood worked in real life his bite wouldn't hurt me. The virus would trigger the shield in my blood cells.

"No, Maddie!" Jack hollered and dashed towards me.

The dull pain from human teeth cut into my neck, followed by a sting in my leg. My head went woozy and I felt my body falling. Numbness eased through my veins and I no longer felt my hands or the chain in them. Alvah was free. Through a blink, I caught him take a bite out of Jack. My last thought:

Success. He first bit me, covered in zombie blood, then Jack. Short blasts rang through the air.

Chapter Twenty-Nine

A dull ache pounded in my neck. I cracked an eye open and visually inspected my surroundings. Four walls and a ceiling, as gray as my disposition. I touched my neck and felt bumps, then remembered Alvah bit me.

"You're awake."

I slid my other eyelid up and glanced in the direction of the voice. "Jack?"

"I was only bringing them to safety."

I slid my arms beneath me and pushed up then slid my back against the wall behind me. Memories slowly came back. That final moment when I was bit and drugged. I rubbed my leg where the sting hit it. It didn't hurt. My family escaped with Sarah and the twins in a Marine vessel. I guessed they knew that now.

"The base is a haven for survivors."

"You betrayed us." The words came out in a slur. I focused on his face then shifted my eyes. From this position I noted we were in tiny rooms. Jack stood, holding bars and staring at me. *How long had he been watching me?*

He shook his head. "I wouldn't do that."

"But you did." My energy was returning and anger was bubbling in my veins.

He shrugged. "It doesn't matter. We only needed you."

"What?" I was confused. Part of it was the drugs wearing off the other part was *why me?*

He sat on the edge of the bed. His hands folded in his lap. "Something about you. The commander needs you to stop the virus or something."

I'd never thought of Jack as intelligent but he had skills that made him useful and occasionally saw the obvious when no one else did but this "commander" did a number on him. There was nothing about me to stop the spread of the disease.

I shook my head. "No, it's not me. I'm just a kid who may be turning into a zombie. That's it." Even though my blood was unique it didn't help anyone but me. Heather hadn't been able to nail down the genes that made my blood special.

He lowered his head. "Bryce is there."

What? Bryce? My brain clicked and I had another question. "Where... Why are we locked in here together?" Maybe he wasn't the big guy on the military campus I assumed he was in Mayport.

"We're in quarantine. We've both been bit. I told them my blood makes anti... bodies."

He said that as if he had no clue what an antibody was. It didn't matter, I let him wonder. "Mine doesn't."

He shifted his eyes towards me. His brows flat. It made his bald head appear more egg shaped. "No."

I'd have to explain this to him. "Your body makes antibodies so you're immune, although I expect you'll get sick first. My body doesn't do that. Heather already tested it. I'm not special just lucky." I lied, flat out lied, but what if my blood cells didn't react like they did in the lab?

202

He swished his mouth to the side as if chewing on an invisible toothpick then stood and paced. "I'm going to get sick?"

"Yes. Remember how my dad got sick? That'll happen to you."

"Sarah didn't when he bit her."

I shrugged. "It was a clean bite. Yours wasn't. I found him with his zombie wife. She'd taken a chunk out of him then blew up. Exploded like a shaken pop." I lifted my hands and spread them for effect. "His mouth was wide open and..." He stared at me expectantly. *Did I have to spell it out?* "Pieces of her went inside his mouth."

His brows formed a V. "He ate her."

"Not on purpose. She blew all over the place. That's what happens to them eventually and I think the virus is released again in the air with it." I wasn't sure about that but it made him think.

"Since he ate some of his wife then bit you, my bite isn't clean and I'll get sick."

I nodded.

"But I have antibodies."

More spelling out. Jeez, he needed a biology lesson to get this one. "Viruses mutate, quickly. That's why getting a flu shot one year doesn't work against every flu and the reason you have to get another the next year. Their DNA changes. That's how species survive. It's called evolution. Your antibodies may not protect you from a mutated version."

He stopped pacing and the lightbulb in his head clicked on. "You made me sick on purpose. You did this!"

My cheesy smile didn't cut it at the moment. "You kidnapped my family."

"No, I didn't. They came willingly and the vessel they left on is military; GPS, it'll bring us straight to them."

The grogginess completely vanished and I realized plain navy blue sweat pants covered my legs and a too-large navy T-shirt hung over my shoulders. "Where're my clothes...?" It wasn't only my clothes. His were changed too. "And yours?"

He dropped on the edge of the bed across from me. "I know we've had our differences but you may have killed me. I could be dead soon."

I tilted my head, wrapped my arms over my chest and glared at him with a 'you didn't answer my question stare'. Really. He needed to get over the we-could-soon-be-zombies thing. It wasn't that I wanted to be one. Not at all, but it was a risk worth taking to save my family that I now guessed didn't exactly need saving.

"They destroyed our clothes."

Oh Jeez, if things could get worse they may have, "How?"

"They incinerate th...em." It really clicked in his head now. "You said the virus was in the air so burning our clothes will send it back into the air."

I nodded. "Maybe. Unless it has a short lifespan outside its host."

He folded his palms around his bald head and shifted on his butt then moved a hand from his head to his butt and pulled something from under it. "I figured maybe you'd want this." He slid my phone across the dull metal floor to me.

There were a few things in this world I kept on me at all times. My phone was one of them. It represented my old life, second was my ax, it represented life, my compass kept Bryce close, and the special bug repellant nail polish protected me from mosquitoes. "Thanks."

"I see you traded the ax for a katana. When did that happen?"

I would still have my ax if it wasn't for everything going south quick in Cape Town. It was still in Ramstein. I wondered if anyone would find it. "I traded it when you traded your soul to the Sith and became *Darth Vader*."

He chuckled and our conversation finally turned to Bryce. According to Jack, he was enjoying the facilities of the base and went willingly. He told me their story; how a soldier found them and Jack used him to get onto the base. He emphasized how they didn't take off the soldier's mask and risk the possibility of exposing him to the sickness. That was a stab at me. Right in my heart. Jack wasn't so bad. In his own way, he thought he was helping.

I flipped my phone from one palm to the other during our discussion then decided what was the harm? I was caught. Pushing in the button, I turned it on.

Chapter Thirty

Bryce

Bryce sat up in bed. They'd taken the straps off and he could roam his confines freely. That was little consolation as the room wasn't larger than ten by ten and lacked a window. He blinked as he stared at the plate of food. A delicious smelling steak, glazed carrots, and an apple.

He picked up the apple and took a bite. He'd eat the carrots too but not the steak, even though his stomach ached for it. Real meat was something he hadn't eaten since the outbreak started and after seeing the zombie shark and rat he wasn't sure meat was safe. However, he'd never seen a zombie plant.

Other than delivering him meals three times a day nobody else had been by his room. No more blood stolen from him. No one to converse with, and no commander. If they'd have asked he would have given them what they needed. He didn't think there was anything to be learned from his DNA or blood but if there was and it helped what was left of humanity he would willingly give anything they needed.

His thoughts shifted to Maddie. He wondered if she'd made it back to Jacksonville. No doubt she'd have an adventure to tell when they met again. He stayed positive and shooed any negative thoughts about her from his head. They would meet again, and soon.

His phone was left with him. That was all he had besides the clothes on his body. Even though he had his phone, they didn't leave him a charger. It didn't matter; there was no one to call. For the fifth time since he'd been locked away he clicked the compass app and was startled when a green light blinked. *Maddie!*

Jack

Maddie lay on her bed staring at her nails. The polish on them chipped and layered funny. It was as if she'd applied a layer over a chipped layer a few times. The mission was to collect her. The commander had tricked him. He now worried about Bryce. *What was special about them anyways?* They were just kids.

In the corner was a crate filled with food and water. No one came in and no one went out during quarantine but after three days with neither of them sick it seemed they should let them out. Instead, no one had come by, as if they'd locked them up and forgotten them.

The boat had stopped some time ago. An hour; maybe longer. He'd gotten used to the hum of the engine and rock of the boat. His years in the Coast Guard came back to him quickly. Each vessel had its own nature. This one was smooth, run on nuclear energy. It was an amphibious assault vehicle with one less amphibian now. That might not go over well with the commander and maybe why he was still locked in the brig with Maddie.

Neither of them had any symptoms, confirming to him that people couldn't be turned zombie from a bite. The man that bit him turned zombie when his wife blew up. The virus was sent back into the air. That was it. He knew there were still many parts of the world the military hadn't gotten to yet. Would the virus spread again when the deaders blew up? He figured it was like a cold. If someone with a cold bit someone else they wouldn't get the cold from that bite but if they sneezed in that person's face they'd get the cold.

He scratched his head and turned his eyes back to Maddie who was now staring blankly at her phone. The click from the door and footfalls caught his attention. Maddie straightened her back and slung her legs over the side of her bed.

He stood and waited at the bars, hoping since they weren't sick after seventy-two hours they were ready to let them out.

A soldier with broad shoulders and the straight build of a man stopped outside their cells. He spoke through the mask on his face. "We picked up a signal, sir."

"Where?" asked Jack, all business-like as if the crew hadn't locked him away in the ship's brig.

"Outer banks of North Carolina. It was from a black box. A plane went down. We don't believe there were any survivors as the plane was in flames."

"Did you search the area anyways?"

"Yes, sir. We didn't find anyone."

"Thank you, um. It's been three days. If we were sick we'd be one of them by now." He figured going about it directly was the answer. After his treatment, the soldier didn't have to come and tell him that. They could have gone about their business. Instead they took the time to inform him.

"I can't let you out, sir, until we get to Norfolk and the doctor clears you, sir."

"I understand." Jack didn't hide the reluctance in his words.

Maddie puffed up. "I don't. We aren't sick! Let us out."

The soldier gave her a quick glance then turned on his heel and marched back up the steps.

Maddie scowled. "What was that?"

"We'll be at the base later today. It won't be long." The hum of the motor told Jack the ship was now moving.

Maddie flopped back onto her bed. By her actions he knew she was upset, angry. Enraged was probably the best word to describe her emotions. The way she lay flat against the mattress with her hands over her head. She was thinking, probably coming up with a plan. That worried him, but there was no way she'd get out of the brig without keys.

Chapter Thirty-One

Maddie

They led me off the ship. Not at gun point, but it felt like it. Might as well have been. I felt their eyes on my head. Like a good little girl, I followed in line. Without any weapons there really wasn't a choice since there was one of me and too many of them. True to Jack's word, the base was surrounded by a giant dome. The sun was bright in the sky and shined into it.

Inside, the temperature of the dome was the coolest I'd felt in months. I guessed about eighty degrees. I knew it was much hotter outside. Norfolk, Virginia was still on the east coast. A few hundred miles or so north of Florida. I knew my science better than geography.

To this point I hadn't looked anyone in the eye. Now my eyes roved the masses. People moved around everywhere, hustling and bustling. I didn't see anyone that resembled Bryce. *If he was here, where?* My phone vibrated in the pocket of the boring sweats they dressed me in. Had people called it when there was no service and now that I was under the dome they were rolling in?

I shielded my eyes and glanced upwards. *What was it made of?* It wasn't glass. That would be stupid, glass shatters and no doubt Norfolk had its share of storms especially being so close to the ocean. Plastic maybe. There was certainly enough on this planet

210

that would never degrade, littering our oceans and land, filling up landfills. I shuddered at the thought. The zombie apocalypse might not have been the worst thing after all. The second time around we could do things right and not destroy the beautiful planet we live on.

I followed the soldier into a long white building with two floors. They stuffed me into another dull room. It looked like an interrogation room seen in movies. The walls were unpainted cement and the only furniture was a chair in the center of it. No windows. I dropped onto the chair and once I was alone I pulled my phone out.

I hope you get this. I see your location. You're not far. Maddie?

I'm locked in a room at the base.

Maddie? I guess your phone is off.

I'm here too, Bryce. I'll look for a way out, I answered and slipped the phone back into my pocket.

All from Bryce. He was locked in a room here like me, but where? The base was large. I searched with my eyes for a way out. There was a large vent in the ceiling, so I pushed the chair beneath it and stood. Even on my tippy toes I wasn't tall enough to reach it. Zombie Girl: highly allergic to mosquitoes and vertically challenged. I sighed. Every superhero had their weakness.

The door rattled and opened. A female soldier walked in with a doctor's mask. Short brown ringlets sprung from around the band that stretched across her face. She didn't have a weapon but the masked individual behind her did. Another man entered the room with a kit. A mask over his mouth too.

"I need a blood sample. It's easier if you don't fight it," the man with the kit said without looking me in the eye. He laid the kit on the floor and fixed a syringe.

Really? I wasn't infected! This had gone too far. I sighed. Maybe it was simply a precaution. I relented and glanced away as he poked my arm. Needles and having my blood drawn always made me queasy. Funny how that worked. I didn't have a problem killing deaders. Yeah, I was grossed out, but didn't get weak in the knees and faint.

I cringed until he took the needle out and taped a band aid over the area. He shot me a quick glance then packed up his kit and they all left. I was alone again. There was no way out of the room and Bryce was as stuck as I was. Not wanting to wear down the battery on my phone, I stuffed it in my pocket and stared at the blank walls, my mind a flutter of activity.

I hoped Heather and Mr. Price were making headway. They were both so close. I didn't exactly know what Bryce's father was working on, only that he was continuing Dr. Stressal's work. *Oh no! How long had she been deader?* It wouldn't matter if she exploded in the lab she was locked in. The virus would be contained as long as they didn't go in or... It was the 'or' that scared me. Or weren't in the room when it happened.

I took a deep breath. I was exposed and my blood shields worked but would their antibodies work too? Since Mr. Price's body had already fought the virus he wouldn't even get sick again but Heather would. She'd never been exposed, only exposed some blood cells in trials and experimentation. They'd be fine. After all, they knew the virus better than anyone.

The dark curly-headed soldier came back into the room. Again she was vacant of a weapon. Maybe I could take her. No, that was a bad idea. If they sent her in without a weapon they didn't consider me a threat. Inwardly, I laughed. Then she spoke, "The commander has questions for you."

I guess taking her out would wait. I had a few questions for the commander. She took me to another room. A man with wild ginger hair and a funky ginger beard sat with his hands folded on the table and an expectant expression on his face. Light streamed in from the window behind him. Bushes, trees, and clumps of grass were his view of the world.

Two chairs sat in front of the thick wooden desk. Light glinted off the bald head of a man in one of the seats. Jack. Jack finally got in his word with the commander. I'd have loved to see that. I knew how fumed Jack was over the isolation they stuck us in for the ride from Florida to Virginia.

I shifted my gaze over the room. No Bryce. *Where was he? Why wasn't he here?*

"Miss Smyth." He scratched behind his ear. "Join us."

I shuffled into the room and the lady soldier closed the door and positioned herself beside it along the wall. It wasn't like I could escape. I mean, I could, but I'd be hard pressed staying hidden in the dome and trying to find a way out.

I had a zillion questions but figured it was better not to let all the eggs out of the basket, as my mom would say, so I let him lead.

"Take a seat, please," the commander insisted.

I didn't want to sit. I wanted to scream and thrust the blade of my katana down his neck but I didn't have it and showing my anger would do no good. In fact it would give him power. I didn't think he needed more with the satisfied twinkle in his eye. I sat.

He leaned forward. Decorations covered his uniform. I wondered if he wore that every day. *Did it make him feel more powerful?* The world we lived in, old positions of authority meant nothing. It was chaos.

"You are an important young woman. I apologize for the uncomfortable ride here. The brig was the only place to hold the two of you. We couldn't take a chance of an outbreak in the confines of the ship."

I glared. *What did he know?* I knew bites didn't spread the disease. I'd known that, but thought a bite from an infected individual who already took a chunk from someone might cause it. I had to rule out the possibility anyways. Evidently not. Jack never even got sick or had symptoms. It was good news.

The commander lowered his brows and leaned back. "I'll get straight to it. We tested your blood as we do with everyone who enters. We have to make sure the pathogen doesn't get in."

From the corner of my eye I watched Jack. A toothpick bobbed in his mouth. He chewed heavy when deep in thought.

The commander continued, "Your blood is clean. You knew that already though. That's why you allowed the zombie to take a chunk from your neck."

The bite was healing nicely by the feel of it, but I hadn't seen it. It could look nasty like Eshe's but I doubted it. If it was infected I'd have a fever. I suppressed the urge to touch it and give him satisfaction.

He stood. "I didn't expect you to be so quiet."

My mind was anything but quiet. It was imagining how I could take him out. A letter opener and a couple pens were stuffed into a jar and a paperweight lay at the edge. It was easily within my reach. I could pick it up and smash his head in. Unfortunately he would move faster than the deaders and my efforts would be thwarted.

I heard the knob turn and the door creak open. I recognized the scent and immediately swung my head over my shoulder.

Chapter Thirty-Two

*B**ryce!* I jumped from my chair, forgetting all about keeping my poker face, and dashed a few steps towards him only to be met with a soldier's gun. I stopped abruptly.

"That brought a reaction," the commander chuckled.

"Jack, why don't you take a stand by Amala and allow Bryce your seat." Jack stood, anger fuming from him. He dropped his mangled toothpick into the trashcan beside the desk and stuffed another one in his mouth. Yeah, he was fuming hot.

Bryce took a seat beside me. We didn't touch, but his presence made my world cheerful, hopeful. It was like now we could conquer anything like we did when we escaped Jacksonville, killed dozens or more deaders, saved our families from a death worse than death; survived a tsunami, a volcano, and now here we sat. I let out a strangled breath.

The commander cleared his throat. "The two of you are special. Your blood is unique. We've tested every survivor we found and none have blood like yours. Many have antibodies. The rest got lucky. That's why we wear the masks."

Bryce interrupted him, "That's why you locked us up. Are we contagious? Are we a threat to the others?" Anger riddled his words.

"No. You are our salvation."

I cut him off. This was too much. My blood couldn't be used. Heather already informed me of

216

that. The answer was in making a vaccine using blood that manufactured antibodies. Our blood was useless to anyone but ourselves. "How do you know any of this?"

He smirked. "We gained access to records from the CDC. This pathogen had already killed several people before the contagion got out. Most importantly, they had detailed records on each of you."

"Us?" I questioned.

"Yes, how often do either of you get sick?"

Sick. I didn't really ever get sick except from mosquitoes. I glanced at Bryce from the corner of my eye. He was more curious than angry. He swallowed. "Not very often," he uttered.

"As in never, except when bit by a mosquito. You see it's very uncommon for anyone to have a fatal allergic reaction to a mosquito bite unless it's infected with a parasite but the two of you had near-death reactions when you were babies. Somehow that reaction triggered something in your blood that protects you from this zombie pathogen."

"There has to be other people in the world that are 'fatally allergic' to mosquitoes."

The commander took his seat and tugged at his ginger beard. "Yes, but we haven't found any that have the same reaction to the virus as the two of you. The CDC thought maybe it was an environmental factor since you were born in the same area only a couple years apart."

The room was silent. *Was that our connection?*

217

Bryce had similar thoughts as he said, "Is that why we shared a dream?"

We were both more curious than angry now. The government kept records on us. *Did they experiment on us? This knowledge opened a new can of worms.*

The commander's brows lowered and parallel lines stretched across his forehead. "Dream?"

We nodded simultaneously, then Bryce spoke, "We shared a dream. In it we saw the apocalypse coming."

"There's nothing about that in their records. I can't say it wasn't engineered by the government but we haven't broken into the FBI, CIA, Homeland Security, or any other acronym yet except the CDC."

Bryce and I glanced at each other.

The door opened behind us again and in walked a lady. Bouncy blonde hair, shaved on the sides, the rest held up in a short ponytail, and vibrant blue eyes the color of the Atlantic. She wasn't more than five feet tall and didn't look older than fifteen.

The commander spoke again, "This is our lead scientist, Marta. She's working on a cure."

Marta smiled. "I don't know anything about infectious diseases. I'm a chemist most known for my line of bug repellant nail polish but I'm doing my best."

Holy flippinoli! She was the Bugbgone Goddess! Bugbgone was the name of the company and she designed a complete line of bug repellant nail polishes in all colors; Skeeter Green, Dragonfly Lavender, Yellow Fly, Blood Tick Red, Wasp

Orange, and so many more. I had most of the colors. I didn't give her a chance to say more when I cut in, "I love your nail polish. It works. I haven't had a mosquito bite since I started wearing it. Other stuff doesn't work as well and I left mine in Jacksonville. Please tell me you can make more here?" The words plummeted from my mouth in one long run-on sentence.

Chapter Thirty-Three

The commander cut in. His nostrils flared in annoyance when he spoke, "As I said, she is the lead scientist. We have a few others on the team as well."

Marta gave me a wink.

Bryce cut in, "If your lead scientist is a chemist. Who else is on the team?"

"Two nurses, a midwife, a phlebotomist, and a college student working on a degree in physics," Marta answered, a tiny sneer in her voice. She definitely had an accent. I assumed Swedish since the company was based out of Falun in Dalarna County.

While I drooled over Marta, Bryce busted out in laughter; after all, where was the biologist, the virologist, or even an entomologist? I burst into laughter and didn't stop until my sides stung and tears rolled from my eyes.

The commander leaned back in his chair, arms over his chest. "Glad you find that entertaining. We work with who we have and the language barriers."

Choking back the lingering chuckles that tickled the back of my throat I asked, "What about Dr. Stressal?"

It turned out they lost contact with her during the hurricane a few weeks ago. That was good. It meant she wasn't exploding too soon. The military didn't know what happened to her, whether she was still working or had died during the storm. Truth was, they were more concerned about finding me and Bryce since we were the answer. The commander had promised her they'd stay away from the facility and so they did.

The door flew open and a young man in civilian clothes ran in. "Commander, we have an emergency. We need you now. Please come."

"Stay here," he ordered us and stormed out.

The room fell silent as our eyes studied each other. I'd had more than enough and figured the only person who'd give me any fight was the female soldier who continued her stance by the door but she was unarmed. "I think I need to see what's so important."

Bryce stepped to my side and wrapped his hand around mine. Together we marched out of the room followed by everyone else. I didn't watch them but counted the footsteps. In the open I took in a long breath of fresh dome air -- then I noticed it.

People were running towards the sides of the dome. It was chaos. Whatever was out there, it was big. My mind envisioned hordes of deaders but if that were the case people wouldn't be flocking to them but away into the center of the base.

"Watch out!" Bryce called and pulled me to his side. We caught each other's gaze as people pushed past us. He saved me from a good trampling. "Come on," he said and dragged me with him.

A human barrier formed around the inside of the dome. I scanned the dome for a place high enough to see above the crowd. When I found it, I squeezed Bryce's hand. "We need to be higher. Can we get up there?" I pointed to what looked like a guard station. From my vantage point, it was unmanned.

He nodded and we doubled back, working our way against the flow and dodging the human traffic. Once we reached the entrance to the guard station. Bryce took the steps two at a time but my legs weren't that long. From the top we could see the entire base. It was completely surrounded. Yachts in the bay, and vans, trucks, and buses surrounded the land as far as my eye could see.

"Look," he pointed, "right past my finger tip."

I slipped my head between his hand and chest. Immediately, I recognized Heather's long dark curls and Deavers' bulky form covered in a blaring white T-shirt with a cowboy hat perched atop his head. Heather and Deavers. Beside them were my parents, Bryce's parents, Sarah, and the twins. A human chain of survivors. *Where did they all come from?*

Bryce wrapped an arm around my waist and pulled me towards him. Our families made it -- and more. Survivors were everywhere. The uneasy feeling in my gut that I'd learned to live with disappeared and the sun seemed to shine brighter. I knew then and there the worst was over and recovery was on its way.

Epilogue

Deavers and his band of misfits found survivors when they island-hopped to fill up on fuel. He'd brought them all to Jacksonville. The plane crash had been a decoy to sneak around the carrier. He and his men chose to join the world military and help survivors.

Heather devised a vaccine using blood that created antibodies. My blood turned out to be useless to anyone but myself. It was administered to everyone who wasn't immune. Bryce's father completed Dr. Stressal's answer to the plague that wiped out most of humanity. A virophage. It was engineered to infect and destroy the living cells containing the virus. With the military's resources, the virophage was released into the air and, through wind and the water cycle, spread throughout the world and the plague was effectively halted. The next batch of lovebugs was small. Each season they grew in numbers but no longer carried the deadly virus.

Heather started a teaching hospital at the base to train people in medicine. Society needed doctors. My father opened up communications and WI-FI across the globe. My mother started a world currency that was more a barter system. Leland Price continued to monitor the environment and engineered ideas to keep our Earth clean of pollution. Katrina and a few other mothers started a school and Jack chose to teach the children self-defense classes. He figured it was a better use of his skills.

We did eventually find two more people with blood like ours in Brazil. It turned out that in order for the blood type to pass on to the next generation both parents had to carry the mutated gene.

No one blamed any individual, corporation, or government for the deader disease. At 7.7 billion people, humans had reached their carrying capacity on Earth. We had a chance to make the planet healthy again and I found a use for the dead. Townships and cities were developed around methane landfills used for generating electricity and the dead were used as fuel. According to the numerologist -- the closest thing we had to one -- they would produce methane for the next thousand years.

It turned out the dome was made of plastic, which gave me an idea. We used the blueprint for it to make domes from recycled plastic around each city. It had a dual purpose. If a deadly plague ever ravaged a city it worked as a quarantine, and if a deadly plague was outside the dome the walls wouldn't allow it in to infect the people. It also made use of the silent plastic epidemic that covered Earth long before the zombies.

All the resources we needed already existed. People from all continents of the world worked together to build a new world. Bryce, Sarah, Mazi, Mesi, and I became explorers and diplomats. We searched for survivors, vaccinated them, and assisted them in building new communities. When trouble from outsiders stirred in the cities we were usually first on the scene.

Marta continued her work and kept me stocked with nail polish. She eventually added body lotion and lip gloss to her line. She even named a new nail color after me. It was a yellow-orange she called 'Zombie Girl'.

We never learned why Bryce and I shared the premonition that put everything into motion, but I never took off my compass. Sometimes there were things that were simply unexplainable.

Message from the author:

When I first moved to Jacksonville, Florida twenty years ago, I encountered my first ever lovebug season. Locals told me they were engineered as an experiment at the University of Florida. I did my research and learned the bugs weren't created as an experiment but migrated from Central and South America. The climate in the southern U.S. suited them and they flourished. All the information provided about them, with the exception of the fictional virus, is true as far as the author knows, based on her research. Any stories you hear about them being an experiment gone wrong is an urban legend… or is it?

lovebugs

About the Author

E lle Klass is the author of mystery, suspense, and contemporary fiction. Her works include *As Snow Falls*, *Eye of the Storm Eilida's Tragedy*, and the *Baby Girl* series. Her work *Eye of the Storm* Eilida's *Tragedy* is a Reader's Favorite Fiction-Paranormal Finalist in the 2015 Reader's Favorite Awards. *Baby Girl Box Set* received Official Honors in Young Adult through New Apple Indie Ebook Awards. She is a night-owl where her imagination feeds off shadows, and creaks in the attic. Visit her website at https://elleklass.weebly.com.

The Vampires Next Door

Prologue

St. Augustine, 1823

Cara shivered, the stone cold floor beneath her. Shrieks sliced through the air above her, echoing through the stone walls. A moldy stench, thick in the surrounding air, drifted up her nostrils. The temperature dropped several degrees as a breeze touched her head. She dared to open her eyes and stare into the darkness surrounding her, peeling one eye open and then the next.

"Cara," sounded a soft voice, almost a whisper. A warm touch caressed her hand, a shadowy figure flashed before her eyes. "You need to leave." The soothing voice didn't elicit fear but warmth and love. Her eyes searched for whom it belonged to. A breeze brushed against her and the voice whispered in her ear. "You need to go. I can lead you."

She tilted her head and gazed upon a transparent woman, no more than twenty. Her flaxen hair fell across her shoulders, circling her heart-shaped face. "Who are you?" Cara stammered.

"I'm Alda, once like you. They've been here for centuries, before the pirates, before the first settlement. The true first inhabitants of this continent."

"Who are they?"

"They are Bloodseekers. Come now!" The urgency in her voice resounded inside Cara. She jumped to her feet and followed the apparition. Alda's white bodice hugged her torso, the black hem grazing the stone floor.

Light from candles illuminated the darkness as they wound through a narrow passageway, as one candle lit ahead of them, the one behind went dark. The brightness of each light cast a glow on the shadow beside it, lighting the faces of each ghost. One apparition after another, men and women, blood drenching their shirts and bodices from the fang marks in their necks. The chilly air sent waves of shivers spiraling through Cara's body. She lifted her arm to touch a girl, no more than twelve, but her hand went through the child's face.

They came upon a fork in the passage, Alda motioned for her to stop. Quickening footsteps sounded from the right. "Plaster yourself against the wall, into the shadows. They see heat, our lack of it will protect you."

Cara did as asked. Not questioning Alda. She knew the footsteps belonged to a Bloodseeker. One had come into her home and killed her family, draining them of every drop of blood. She tried to escape, to run, but he was too quick. His dark eyes bored into hers. And a voice inside her head commanded her to stop. Her body froze in place. She tried to move but his mind controlled the core of her brain and she collapsed, waking up on the stone floor.

Her mind swarming back to the present, she pressed herself against the wall, the shadowy apparitions swarmed around her, blanketing her in darkness, shielding her from the Bloodseeker. His footsteps halted at the fork, as if deliberating which direction to go. He turned and followed the corridor leading to the room she'd left, he halted. His black eyes glowed through the shadows surrounding her. She closed her eyes tight, to avoid his mind commands and held her breath. Cara stayed as motionless as possible, controlling the tremors threatening to shake her body.

Her sense of hearing heightened with her eyes squeezed shut, she heard his footsteps walk away from her and continue through the corridor. She popped her eyes open and watched his form through the corner of her eye. When he disappeared around the corner, Alda motioned for her to follow. *He'd know she wasn't there. He'd look for her.* The apparitions parted as Cara moved away from the wall.

Alda floated up the stairwell as Cara followed with gentle footsteps, careful not to draw his attention. A wooden door appeared before Cara as she reached the top of the stairs. Alda motioned for her to open it, the hinges creaking as she pushed it.

Moonlight from the crescent moon streamed through the parted heavy curtains, bathing the room in enough light that Cara could see. Dozens of ghosts swarmed the room. Now, able to see them clearly, she gasped. Their skin tones and origins varied - black, white, and varying shades of brown. None older than her. Their styles of dress told her many lived centuries before her. A young black ghost hovered in front of her, clothed in a thick graying dress. Her gentle brown eyes sent a burst of warmth through Cara's quaking, goose-pimpled body.

Alda soared towards a bookshelf and pointed to a nondescript brown leather book. "Pull it."

Cara hurried towards the shelf and lifted the book, the shelf easing back to reveal another room.

"Take the book inside the room. The door will close behind you."

Cara didn't argue. Thundering sets of footsteps pounded the floor behind her, only moments from catching her she dived into the room. The book case closed, leaving behind all the ghosts except Alda. A Bloodseeker rushed towards it, catching it with his hand. He forced the heavy door open. Cara scooted away from his grasp.

A bright red light flickered from the corner of the dark room. "Grab the light!" Alda yelled. Cara scurried towards it, dropping the book as she reached for it. She held it firmly in her hand and tugged, but the object was caught on something she couldn't see in the dark.

The Bloodseeker dived for her, catching her other arm in his firm grasp. A blast of white light diffused through the room from the object Cara clutched in her hand. He pulled her towards him. She tightened her grasp as the object and the nail it was stuck on slackened from the wall. The

Bloodseeker, too late to stop her, screamed in agony as the light blasted him against the door, his body engulfed in flames.

The light enveloped Cara, pushing its way through her body. She burst into fire, the flames licking the walls, then eddying into nothingness. Her ginger hair now crimson red, her amber eyes shining as garnets in the darkness. Beneath her skin, muscles exploded to the surface.

"What's happening?"

A smile widened on Alda's face. "You're the one. We've waited for you."

"What do you mean and how come I can see you and they can't?"

"You are a Slayer, that's why you see us. As long as you wear the amulet you will be indestructible and invisible to the Bloodseekers. They won't be able to harm you. Your job is to find others like yourself and slay every last Bloodseeker. Don't ever take it off and keep it protected beneath your clothes. Should it fall into their hands they will use it against you. You see us because you are special. All the answers are in the book. Take it, place the amulet around your neck and leave now!"

Cara leaned over and grabbed the book. She then pulled the glowing amulet over her head. "What about you and the others?"

"You have freed us. We are forever grateful but you must leave."

Cara hurried towards the door, stepping on the Bloodseeker's ashes. The door opened for her and she ran through the house, ghosts guiding her way.

She dodged the Bloodseekers, their dark glowing eyes searching, fangs sharp as daggers protruding from their upper gums. Their blood covered mouths saturated the air with the scent of iron. Claw-like fingers sliced through the air, scratching her clothes as she sprinted past them, hurdling tables and furniture with skill and agility unknown to her.

Finally, reaching the front entrance, she twisted the golden knob on the large, chunky door and ran into the morning's first light. Dawn. The sun rising just above the horizon. She stepped onto the porch, Bloodseekers on her trail. Stumbling down the steps, she landed face first in the dirt. Scrambling she lifted herself upright and quickly turned towards the house.

A tall, thin Bloodseeker hissed, shielding his face as he sank into the house, flames licking his hands. The sun's light rose bigger and brighter in the sky, immersing the house in radiance. The ground shook. She sprinted.

Reaching the relative safety of the tree line, she turned in time to watch the ground part around the house, swallowing it. Thousands of lights glowed as the ghosts swirled into the atmosphere, rising high into the sky as they disappeared. Screams reverberated in the air surrounding her as the Bloodseekers were burned and buried.

She cupped her ears and knelt, curling her head towards her knees to muffle their death screeches. Unable to stifle the noise, tears rose to her eyes from the pain in her throbbing ears. As soon as the screeching began, it stopped, and the earth filled in above the house. The ground appeared undisturbed. The sun shone high in the sky, erasing the dreadful night.

Cara lifted the amulet hanging against her chest, a large red stone set in the center surrounded by, and hanging on, a silver chain. She clutched it, the book tucked beneath her arm, and marched down the road. Not a soul peered outside their windows or took notice of the event.

The house was wiped from existence and erased from St. Augustine's inhabitants' minds. Cara's secret.

Chapter 1

Alison

Music surging from the apartment next door startled Alison awake. Her body rolled off the couch with a soft thump, landing on an assortment of throw pillows she'd kicked off during her nap. She pulled herself off the floor and rubbed the sleep from her eyes. Mouth dry as the Sahara, she headed towards the kitchen for water. A shrill female scream vibrated against her eardrums, causing her to jump and drop her empty tumbler. It crashed to the floor with a loud thunk, mimicked by the shattering glass outside her front door.

The apartment complex was always quiet, especially after dark. It had to be the new neighbors. After sunset, they'd moved into the adjoining apartment. As a lonely girl in a new city, she'd watched them with admiration. Two women, neither over the age of twenty-five, single women living on their own. One with long, brown wavy hair and eyes bluer than any she'd seen before. A surreal blue. The other girl had blonde highlights throughout the light brown hair, framing her flawless face and intense green eyes. Both had curves in the right places.

Self-conscious, she had compared her still developing body to their mature ones. Her gut swelled over her sweatpants and her chest had barely sprouted. She wore an A-cup to make herself feel better, but really she didn't think anyone noticed when she went braless. At the moment her admiration for them plummeted; beautiful or not, they were an annoyance!

Two voices, one female the other male, argued in the breezeway, the open air hallway between the apartments, upsetting her, but also piquing her natural teenage curiosity. She peered through the peephole hoping to catch sight of someone in the breezeway between the apartments but all she saw was the apartment across the hall. Her own front door blocking the view of the adjoining apartment.

"I hate you!" Then the door slammed so hard it made the walls tremble and the door shake. Alison's face pressed against the door, she yelped from the jolt against her nose. Rubbing it, she moved away and strolled back to the kitchen, picked up her tumbler and poured filtered water into it, drinking it all in several successive gulps. Catching her breath she considered her options. She could knock on their door and ask them nicely to lower their music or she could wait it out.

Home alone, as her mother worked as a nurse at Flagler hospital, and hundreds of miles from her father and best friend, she was unsure what to do, but didn't feel knocking on the door was the best choice. Actually, the idea freaked her out. Instead, she padded to the coffee table, picked up her tablet and checked the time. She was overly dismayed when her tablet screen displayed eleven p.m.

A tad scared but nosy and irritated, she slid the patio door open and listened, maybe they were wrapping up the party. All she heard was murmuring half-drowned by the music. Upset, lonely and slightly frightened she sent her BFF in Virginia a message: *I hate my life. New neighbors are crazy. I miss you.* She knew Vicky was asleep like normal people and wouldn't see her message for several more hours.

Alison laid her phone on the table and gazed towards the heavens. A chunk of moon peeked out from the surrounding clouds. Always interested in lunar phases as most paranormal books she read featured the moon was an important piece of the story, and each phase having a specific meaning. The most well-known were the werewolves who morphed during a full moon, but red moons and blue moons had meanings too. Her body shuddered as the party next door continued, but the steady purr of a familiar vehicle kept her plastered to the chair.

Within seconds an emerald green Charger hugged the road as it passed her screened patio. Her eyes moved with it as the driver swung around the curve. She jumped from the plastic patio chair, grabbed her phone, her heart beating fast within her chest, and with a sigh, stepped inside. Almost forgetting her troublesome new neighbors. She slid the heavy glass door closed, bolting all the locks and tugging to be sure.

She raced toward the dining room window and parted the blinds, a large breezeway with philodendrons planted in the middle separated the apartments. She recognized the emerald green Dodge Charger and its driver, Rodham. To her, his chiseled body screamed for every teenage girl in a fifty mile radius to pay attention. He lived kitty corner to her apartment and directly across the hall from the new, loud neighbors.

He rounded the corner of the building, keys jingling in his hands, eyes shooting a glance across the hall towards the partying neighbors' apartment. Well defined muscles on his forearm bulged as he twisted the key in the lock. She imagined herself wrapped in those arms, his full lips kissing her neck and drifting behind her ears. Still a virgin with no prospects or past boyfriends, thoughts of Rodham filled her waking and sleeping mind. Under no circumstances did she think a hot, dreamy creature like Rodham would date an ordinary, overweight, ginger like her because she lacked the talent and looks to suck men into her web. Rodham closed the door and her moment of teenage lust ended.

Dropping the blinds, she sauntered to the fridge and lifted the papers hung on the fridge with magnets, searching for an emergency number for the apartment complex. Her mother was organized, down to every detail. As the thought brushed through her mind, she glanced at the pillows still lying on the floor and made a mental note to pick them up before bed.

With a triumphant grin, she found the number and lifted it off the fridge. Loud neighbors at eleven p.m. was an emergency in her book. She dialed the number and it directed her to leave a message. *What if I was dying? What if someone broke in and I was shivering in terror in my closet? Whatever,* she shrugged and left a message, tossed the pillows onto the couch and crawled into bed, drawing the comforter over her head, and sticking in her earbuds. She turned up the volume, attempting to drown the commotion next door and opened her tablet to her current book, *City by the Bay*.

Thirty minutes later a pounding on the front door interrupted her reading, and a shudder ran down her spine. She curled further under her covers like a frightened turtle inside its shell.

Rodham

A bottle cap skittered across the cement breezeway as Rodham rounded the corner. It landed in the dirt next to a philodendron leaf. A shattered glass bottle twinkled in the lights, its contents sprayed across the cement wall, puddling on the concrete beneath. The heavy beat from the music across the hall thumped against his eardrums.

When he drove past the apartment, he captured a glimpse of the new neighbors. Several people stood on the patio, each holding drinks in their hands. The sliding glass door open, he saw into their apartment, where a woman with blondish hair danced against a dark haired man. Her back rubbing his chest, she slid down him, her flowing hair trailing across his torso. Her partner leaned his face towards hers as she grabbed a handful of his dark hair.

Rodham fumbled with the lock, aware the
apartment across the hall was empty when he'd left
with his friend, Adrian, for Daytona to surf. Now,
new, annoying neighbors partied and littered the
breezeway. He wondered how the quiet ginger next
door was faring against the noise. Always aloof with
her tablet in front of her face - at the beach, the
pool, slung in a hammock on the shore of the
manmade lake at the apartment complex.

Her amber eyes mysterious and deep, ginger hair
trailing her back with gentle waves falling across her
shoulders, freckles kissed her porcelain cheeks.
Intent on her tablet, she always twisted stray strands
between her fingers. From the corner of his eye he
caught her amber eyes peering from her parted
blinds, biting her natural cherry colored bottom lip,
watching as he hurried and closed the door, locking
out the new, annoying neighbors.

One finger pushed against his ear, his cell phone
meshed against his other, Rodham's father
acknowledged he was home with a quick flash of his
eyes, then he squinted and bent over talking to the
person on the other end of the line.

His mom sat, feet propped on the coffee table
and plugs in her ears. Her back against the soft
cushion of the sectional. Closed captioning jogged
across the TV screen. She waved at him as he
disappeared into his room. Beach sand stuck to
every part of his body, he gathered clean clothes and
rushed into the shower.

He allowed the warm water to wash the sand
down the drain, the cute ginger filling his thoughts.

Fully focused on her, a set of dagger-tipped fangs interrupted his thoughts. A single drop of blood hung in the air as it fell from the point of a fang. A thunderous knock blasted him out of the vision. Catching the shower's side handle to keep from slipping, he knocked the back of his head against the tile wall, hard enough to give him a temporary headache. He scurried out of the shower, both his parents' were watching something through the parted blinds.

Chapter 2

Alison

Alison yanked the earbuds out of her ears and listened. The knocking stopped, the music stopped, and muffled voices drifted through the wall. Throwing off her covers, she hurried towards the dining room window, attempting to catch a glimpse. All she saw was the black-clothed, burly back of a police officer scolding her neighbors.

"We've had complaints. This is a residential area and we're going to have to ask you to keep your music down," the officer said in a deep voice.

Across the hall, Rodham's ebony face appeared through parted blinds. His sable eyes met her amber orbs locking them in a gaze. *He noticed me!* Thought Alison, the ambiguous girl whom he hadn't paid one ounce of attention to all summer. Warmth tingled through her body and she all but forgot about her matted bed-head, and Tinker Bell pajamas. The expanded-second locked gaze ended, and he dropped his blinds back in place.

She twirled her body away from the window and, in a dreamy state, leaned against the wall, thoughts of the day she followed him to the beach, flitted through her head. She'd poised her chair under an umbrella, sprayed SPF 130 over her entire pale body, placed a floppy hat on her head and watched him with stars in her eyes from behind the pages of her book while pretty girls with dream bodies in their bikinis flocked towards him like bees to honey. His brown skin velvet beneath the sun. She pushed her book, *Beyond the Hidden Sky*, over her face and read, catching glimpses of Rodham. In her one-piece with a baggy T-shirt to cover her jelly stomach she didn't think she compared to the other teens.

She peeled herself off the wall and strolled to her bedroom. *He noticed me!* Sinking into her bed she savored our moment in her mind, silence next door - she fell asleep.

Sun filtering through her window awoke her the following morning. She crept towards her mother's room, peeking around the corner of her opened door. She lay on her bed, burrito-wrapped inside the covers, feet poking out the end. Alison sighed relief that her mother was home. She'd grown used to her absence at night and had felt safe enough until last night.

Her stomach grumbling for food, she strolled into the kitchen, poured a bowl of cereal and ate while she turned on her tablet and continued reading her current book.

Hours later, her mother stretched her arms as she exited her bedroom and ambled into the kitchen. With a yawn she said, "Good afternoon, sweetie."

Peeling her eyes from her tablet and current fictional world, Alison acknowledged her mother from her prone position on the couch and lifted her eyes responding, "Hi, Mom. I fixed lunch, frozen lasagna and garlic bread."

"What did I ever do to get such a wonderful daughter?" She spied Alison's tablet. "I love all the reading you do. It helps the mind grow, but I hate seeing you inside all day, every day. That's why we bought you the car so you could get out, explore your new surroundings, meet new people. This is St. Augustine, the oldest city in the U.S., there's more than enough to keep you busy and entertained." She gently pushed Alison's legs towards the back cushion of the couch and sat, pecking her on the cheek.

Alison's parents had bought her a 2000 Corolla, not a bad first car. In fact, she thought it was an excellent first car - everything worked. The problem was they lived in Florida and she detested starting the car and setting the air conditioning to full blast for ten minutes before she could sit in it without melting or touch the steering wheel without second degree burns.

Her next problem was the friend issue. As an introverted book nerd, it took her years to build the relationships she had - Vicky, she was it. Her only friend. She anticipated she'd be spending the two years left of high school alone.

Alison's phone vibrated and she glanced at the message, Vicky responding to her late night text. *Miss you! Talk later, school shopping.* She wished she was in Virginia shopping with her, the way they'd done the past few years, since their parents deemed them old enough to wander the mall without 24/7 parental supervision.

"I miss Vicky, my high school, the mountains, the cooler night air."

Her mother sighed and brushed her hand through Alison's hair. "Honey, I know this is difficult for you. But your dad travels a lot. I was offered a job here. This is our home now. School starts next week, try and make friends."

"I know. I'll try." She bit her lower lip. "And when the weather gets cooler I'll explore the city." After her parents' divorce, her mother, who'd spent sixteen years as a stay at home mom, dusted off her nursing degree and sent her resume all over the U.S., hoping to land a job. She did, in St. Augustine, to Alison's bad fortune.

Her mother stood and wandered towards the kitchen, cutting a slice of lasagna and placing it on a plate, then sighed as she popped it in the microwave. "I've been working a lot, paying moving expenses. Once they're paid up we'll do more exploring together."

Facing away from her mother, Alison rolled her eyes and shrugged, the only exploring they'd done together was watching an IMAX movie at World Golf Village. And it was an excellent outing but, other than that, her mother constantly worked. Alison was old enough to understand child support didn't pay everything. She also understood her parents continued an amiable relationship if nothing else than for her, and her father would do more to help them out. Her mother, proud and stubborn, refused any money other than the court dictated amount.

She contemplated telling her mother about the neighbors but chose against it, assuming it was a one-night thing.

As soon as the sun went down, the neighbors' thumping music and partying began, growing louder as the night progressed. She built up the nerve to walk to her front door, replaying what she would say in her mind. As she turned the knob she chickened out, her anger inside recoiled and she stuck her earbuds in and read instead.

After midnight a thump hit her bedroom wall, she leaped off the couch in response. The decorative Asian fan above the couch shifted. Several more thumps followed, sounding like a body thrown against the wall. She stood in the doorway, expecting someone to burst through the wall any second. A shrill banshee scream shuddered through the air, piercing her eardrums, and vibrating through her head. In pain, Alison crumpled to the ground, holding her head between her hands.

Frozen in pain, she gripped the floor and dragged her body along it to the couch, reached her hand onto the cushion and fumbled for her phone. Then the noise stopped. Her fingers brushed against her phone and she snatched it up. Poised on the floor, she scrolled through her short phone log and redialed the emergency number then buried herself into the couch, encasing her fear-shivering body in a throw blanket.

Rodham

At the same moment, in his room playing Wii, a primitive wail sliced through the music, ringing in Rodham's ears. He doubled in pain, and curled into a ball, dropping the video game controller from his hand.

When the noise subsided, Rodham collected himself. Unable to shrug it off, he contemplated where the noise originated. Thoughts of his strange neighbors and the odd events, including his strange visions, circulated in his head.

In the living room, he joined his parents. Their eyes fixed on the TV as they watched a movie, closed captioning scrolling across the screen. Noticing her son's befuzzled look, his mother asked, "Everything OK?"

He shifted his eyes to hers. "Did you hear that?"

His father chuckled. "Two nights in a row. I've already called the sheriff and will make a complaint at the office in the morning."

Rodham shrugged and leaned back into the recliner, convinced his parents didn't hear the shrill scream or couldn't hear it over the pulsating music. In science class he learned that young adults were capable of hearing frequencies adults ears couldn't.

Within a half hour a police officer knocked on their neighbor's door, read them the "be quiet" act and the noise stopped.

The following two nights, the neighbors' partying after sunset continued. Determined to understand the strange sequence of events, Rodham slipped upstairs to the second floor balcony, found a dark corner and waited. He wanted to know, see everything. His visions and the noise told him something was very wrong. No matter how absurd it sounded, even inside his own head, his curiosity drove him forward.

The crackle of the police radio hummed before he saw the two officers. Within moments a female officer with a blonde bob cut and wide hips, along with a male, his paunchy gut swelling over his pants, rounded the corner. The man slipped a piece of chewing gum into his mouth, stuffing the wrapper into his pants and chomped, his high and tight hair style moved up and down with the motion.

They knocked on the door and a woman with blonde highlights contrasting against her brown hair opened it. She leaned against the door frame, her long legs flowing like silk from her short denim skirt. "Hello officers."

"Ma'am, four nights in a row we've been called to this location for the same reason. I think we need to have a discussion with you and your roommate." His head bobbed as he glanced around her at the inside of the apartment. From Rodham's position he couldn't see inside but not willing to give away his position, he stayed put.

A crooked, sinister smile crossed her oval face, and she waved the officers inside. Her eyes darted right then left, scoping the breezeway before she closed the door.

In the dark corner, Rodham waited. The music stopped, but he never saw the police leave. Fear rushed against his spine, and he leaped down the stairs, taking two at a time, and thrust his front door open. His parents looked at him wearing identical expressions of puzzlement. He ignored them, locked the door, and parted the blinds enough to peek out with one eye.

"What's going on?" questioned his father, as he walked towards him.

"Police are here again, two of them tonight. They went inside the apartment."

"Young, irresponsible, spoiled girls is all. Their parents probably pay for the apartment to get them out of their own home." He harrumphed. "Now that the noise has stopped we're heading to bed."

"Goodnight, don't stay up too late," called his mother as she trailed to bed.

"Goodnight," answered Rodham, his eye still fixated on the apartment across the hall.

He knew from the tone in his father's voice he questioned his actions, but not enough to figure them out after four near-sleepless nights.

Their neighbor's blinds were parted slightly, allowing him to see the woman with highlighted hair, the one who opened the door, stared into the male officer's eyes and brushed her fingers against his neck. She opened her mouth, fangs erupted from her gums. Rodham's eyes widened as he watched the man's blood vessels bulge from beneath his skin and pulsate as his blood pumped through his arteries. She tilted her head and sunk her fangs into his flesh, a drop of blood trailed down his neck, and under his shirt.

Her eyes shifted towards Rodham, who stumbled backwards and blinked his eyes, the blinds falling into place. His heartbeat steady and fast inside his chest and he struggled to catch his breath.

www.ingramcontent.com/pod-product-compliance
Lightning Source LLC
Chambersburg PA
CBHW060349030726
47497CB00003B/657